"What's your idea of the perfect date?" Ella asked.

The change in topic was so sudden it made Josh's head spin.

He studied her as the question pinged through his mind, and he discovered with a surprise that his answer wouldn't be what he'd expected.

Several strands of shiny hair had escaped the knot at the back of her head, and her face was flushed with color, whether from embarrassment or the heat that sparked between them, Josh didn't know.

But he very much wanted to because, at the moment, any perfect date he imagined involved this woman, which could not end well for either of them.

"I guess a nice dinner and good conversation."

"Basic," she muttered.

He rubbed a hand along the back of his neck and willed away the heat he could feel rising to his cheeks. "There's nothing wrong with basic, and why do you care? Anna was asking me weird questions earlier. What's the deal, Ella?"

She snagged her plump lower lip with her teeth, and awareness zinged through him. If she was trying to distract him, she'd picked a perfect way.

"I'm going to help you find a wife."

Dear Reader,

Books are like children—it's almost impossible to pick a favorite. But sometimes a story feels special from the beginning, and that's how I felt with *A Starlight Summer*.

No one from Ella Samuelson's hometown understands why she suddenly gave up her career as a globe-trotting pediatric nurse for an international health-care organization to return to Starlight and take on a series of random jobs, and Ella has no intention of explaining herself. From the day her mother died when she was a teenager, Ella became a master of compartmentalizing her feelings, unwilling to show any emotion that might leave her vulnerable and weak. But one summer when she's a camp counselor in Starlight, a precocious little girl and her gentle father will push Ella to the point where her heart either breaks in two or is healed for good.

Josh Johnson learned all about heartbreak after his ex-wife left him and his six-year-old daughter, Anna, when the young girl was diagnosed with cancer. Dealing with a divorce and a sick child on his own made Josh wary of trusting anyone, but Anna has been healthy for nearly two years, and he's trying to rebuild their lives and regain the hope he once had for his future.

Although the attraction that sparks between Josh and Ella when their paths cross sends his heart and his body into overdrive, it's clear she doesn't have plans to stick around Starlight long term. Josh won't risk his daughter being deserted again. Yet spending time with Ella helps heal the broken places inside him.

I hope you enjoy reading Josh and Ella's story as much as I loved writing it!

Hugs,

Michelle

A Starlight Summer

MICHELLE MAJOR

HARLEQUIN
SPECIAL
EDITION

Recycling programs
for this product may
not exist in your area.

ISBN-13: 978-1-335-40860-0

A Starlight Summer

Copyright © 2022 by Michelle Major

For questions and comments about the quality of this book,
please contact us at CustomerService@Harlequin.com.

Harlequin Enterprises ULC
22 Adelaide St. West, 41st Floor
Toronto, Ontario M5H 4E3, Canada
www.Harlequin.com

Printed in U.S.A.

Michelle Major grew up in Ohio but dreamed of living in the mountains. Soon after graduating with a degree in journalism, she pointed her car west and settled in Colorado. Her life and house are filled with one great husband, two beautiful kids, a few furry pets and several well-behaved reptiles. She's grateful to have found her passion writing stories with happy endings. Michelle loves to hear from her readers at michellemajor.com.

Books by Michelle Major

Harlequin Special Edition

Welcome to Starlight

The Best Intentions
The Last Man She Expected
His Secret Starlight Baby
Starlight and the Single Dad

Crimson, Colorado

Anything for His Baby
A Baby and a Betrothal
Always the Best Man
Christmas on Crimson Mountain
Romancing the Wallflower
Sleigh Bells in Crimson
Coming Home to Crimson

Maggie & Griffin

Falling for the Wrong Brother
Second Chance in Stonecreek
A Stonecreek Christmas Reunion

Visit the Author Profile page
at Harlequin.com for more titles.

To Joellyn and Jess. I'm inspired by your strength.

Chapter One

It was a brilliant day in Starlight, Washington, the sky a singular blue that marked a perfect summer afternoon. Dazzling and intense without a wisp of a cloud marring the meteorological perfection.

Ella Samuelson was in the mood to hit something.

She thought it a benefit that she wanted to take out her temper on a poor, unsuspecting inanimate object and not an actual living person.

That showed a surfeit of maturity and self-control, right?

Too bad she couldn't get a handle on her emotions as quickly as she could control her urges.

She stood at the edge of the crowd at the weekend festival that paid tribute—in large part—to her late mother's devotion to supporting the arts in the picturesque town nestled at the base of the Cascade Mountains. Ella should feel happy.

At least she should be able to muster satisfaction and pride.

She'd just announced the recipients of the artist stipend funded by her family's bank. Her father had begun supporting the creative community in Starlight, and specifically this summer art festival, shortly after his wife's death to honor her memory.

It was a noble endeavor, but noble hadn't mattered to a teenage Ella, who'd lost her gentle and patient mother in a tragic car accident. Ella and her older brother, Finn, who'd been in the car with their mom at the time of the wreck, had been devastated. Their father, Jack, was gutted by grief and emotionally walled himself off from his kids for years just at the time when they needed him the most.

Ella had felt deserted, heartbroken and angry. She'd rebelled in the usual ways of angsty teenage girls, embarrassed now that she hadn't even been able to find a creative outlet for her feelings. Instead, she'd anesthetized herself and shoved them down and run from her emotions. Run from everything that reminded her of home.

At least she'd parlayed the running into a successful career as a traveling nurse. But she'd managed to bungle that as well, when the pressure of facing illness, death and trauma in remote and war-torn regions of the world had become too much.

When her emotions refused to be pushed down any longer, she'd ended up weeping and eventually nearly catatonic on the floor of a mud hut in a speck of a village on the outskirts of a South American jungle.

She'd returned to her hometown under the guise of taking a break and reconnecting with her dad and brother after finding out about her father's cancer diagnosis. The big C had been an excuse to run once more.

Two months of a planned break had turned into nearly two years in Starlight. She still hadn't been able to return to the nursing profession that had once been her calling. At the moment, she worked odd jobs around town and barely scraped together enough money to afford rent now that she'd moved out of her dad's guesthouse. Her pride remained easier to deal with than emotions, and Ella had pride in spades.

She'd made a deal with one of her high school friends for reduced rent on a short-term lease if she helped to fix up the guy's ramshackle duplex so he could sell it once she left town. She was leaving town and had finally given herself a deadline.

The end of the summer.

She'd agreed to return to the traveling nurses'

agency she previously worked for, although she hadn't yet signed the official contract. Still, they were expecting her to report for duty on the first of September.

The thought of getting on a plane and flying to someplace where they urgently needed medical staff made Ella's chest knot so tightly it was a wonder she could breathe.

The alternative, which her new friends suggested on a regular basis, was staying in Starlight. Put down roots and admit she wanted the kind of steady life her parents had before her mother's death. But Ella didn't trust it. She knew from experience that stable didn't equate to safe. Why not push the envelope and tempt the adventure gods as much as she could?

What was the worst that could happen?

"You're scaring the small children with that frown," a deep voice said near her ear.

She resisted the immediate urge to offer a one-fingered salute in response. There were families with young kids milling about as they'd reached the point in the festival when the committee was giving out the youth awards.

She cocked her head ever so slightly to see Josh Johnson at her side, wearing one of his trademark faded flannels despite the warm temperature. The muted pattern seemed to accentuate skin burnished by the sun and the scruffy five-o'clock shadow that roughened his strong jaw.

"If it keeps the little ankle biters at bay, then I'm doing something right," she told him as she returned her attention to the speaker. "Shouldn't you be off impressing adoring moms with your juggling or leaping tall buildings in a single bound or whatever it is Superdads do on the weekend?"

Josh chuckled—a deep rumble that had a surprising bite to it. An edge Ella found appealing even though she knew there was nothing for her when it came to this particular man.

She'd lapsed into quite a dry spell since returning to Starlight. If she were going to pick a guy to break it, Josh would be at the bottom of that list. He would be on a different pad of paper entirely. A completely foreign language to the one Ella spoke.

She'd known Josh in high school, but they hadn't run in the same circles. He was far too pleasant for her. Ella hadn't been a fan of nice guys back in the day. Not much had changed in that respect. Josh's inherent kindness, open smile and willingness to pitch in whenever someone needed help around town made him genuinely beloved in the close-knit Starlight community. And a man who wasn't for her. Josh was the very picture of steady and stable, and Ella was a runner at heart.

Which did not account for the awareness that

sizzled along her skin as he playfully nudged her elbow.

Okay, the guy was cute enough—even she could admit that. With his dark hair and big soulful brown eyes, he was like a warm hug personified.

Ella reminded herself that she didn't like cuddling.

"Let me guess," she said as she scanned the children crowded in front of the stage. "Anna is getting an award?"

He nodded and didn't bother to hide his proud grin. "My mom gave her an old camera for her eighth birthday, and she's got some natural talent for a kid her age."

"Of course," Ella murmured. "Takes after her father—perfect in every way."

"Tough crowd." Josh let out an amused snort. "It's no secret you don't like my kid or me, although neither of us is perfect."

"I didn't say either of those things," Ella countered, embarrassment making her cheeks heat. What kind of a person wouldn't like an adorable girl who'd survived a bout with leukemia and her devoted father? Apparently, someone like Ella who had a scrap of tin where her heart should be. "I like Anna just fine."

Josh's smile widened, and his good humor in the face of Ella's acerbic attitude only made him more appealing—and more annoying.

"You're a terrible liar."

"Trust me. I'm a fantastic liar. You have no idea." She laughed, but when he didn't seem to appreciate the joke, Ella's stomach felt squirmy, like it was filled with a million creepy-crawlies. She didn't exactly broadcast the fact that she was faking much of her happiness and any sense of contentment she exuded.

It was disconcerting to think that Josh Johnson, a man who was her polar opposite in every discernible way, would be the one to see right through her defenses.

Her sister-in-law, Kaitlyn, who was doing emcee duties for the awards ceremony, announced Anna Johnson's name along with the other winners.

Josh took a step forward, clapping and whistling for his daughter and giving Ella a perfect view of his broad shoulders and strong back. His thick hair curled around his collar like he needed a cut but had forgotten to make an appointment at the barber.

Ella could imagine any number of women who'd like to step in and help manage his busy life while warming his bed—she'd guess it was a big one— in the process.

Not her. Not with Josh.

So why did reminding herself that they weren't a fit make her chest ache again?

No point in examining that unwelcome thought

any closer, Ella decided. While everyone else focused on the kids, she turned away.

An hour later, she walked toward a quiet section of the grassy town square, down a path surrounded on both sides by rows of boxwoods and bright flowers along the borders.

This area had been established almost a decade earlier, commissioned by her father as another tribute to his late wife.

Ella's mother had loved the story *The Secret Garden*, and her dad funded these plantings and the sculpture at the center of this space in honor of her mom's memory. He'd sent pictures to her and her brother, Finn, when the area had been dedicated. Neither of them had returned to Starlight for the ceremony.

Finn was different now. In his own way, he'd made peace with their father and had taken his rightful place heading up the bank that had been in their family for several generations.

Ella might have picked Starlight as the place to shove her head in the sand against the problems of her life, but she wasn't quite ready to play nice.

To that end, she purposely hadn't visited this part of the town square. It would have given her father too much satisfaction, she told herself.

The absolute truth might have been that she was already assailed by memories of her mother in this town and her heart. She hadn't wanted to face the reminder of her death. She didn't need a garden statue to remember Katie Samuelson.

But she could no longer stay away. She needed resolution with the past before she left Starlight to claim her future once and for all.

As she approached, Ella heard the sound of a young girl's voice speaking in conversational tones, although no one talked back to her. It was ridiculous for Ella to feel as though she were intruding on some private moment. This was her mother's memorial, after all. Although she'd kept her distance until now, suddenly she felt the need to see the statue that had been forged to commemorate her mother's spirit.

Her steps slowed as she caught sight of the girl with dark wavy hair and a sunset-pink dress. Anna Johnson held up the ribbon she'd won earlier as if the bronze statue she faced was a real person.

"And Daddy says that for Christmas I can ask Santa for a new lens, but I think Nana will get me one now if I talk to her. I like the blue ribbon, especially because Mariah Corcoran only got a red one. She made fun of me when my hair fell out, and Mommy called her the B-word. That was before Mommy left."

Darn it.

Ella rubbed two fingers against her chest. The last thing she needed was to feel tenderness toward a kid whose father she wanted to avoid. Where was he, anyway?

She didn't want the reminder that Josh's daughter had not only endured childhood cancer, but the girl's mother had walked out on her family just as Anna was finishing her treatment.

Talk about a B-word.

Ella must have said the words out loud because Anna whirled toward her, dropping her ribbon onto the gravel path in her surprise.

"You can't be here," the girl said, scowling as she bent to pick up the ribbon. "This is my place."

"This is a public park," Ella pointed out, "and I most certainly have a right to be here." She moved forward slowly, studying the sculpture as she did. "That's my mother."

Anna's rosebud mouth opened in shock as she looked between Ella and the sculpture, which bore a striking resemblance to Katie Samuelson.

Although formed out of bronze, Ella could see the kindness of her mother in it. The woman's head bent toward the two children who sat at her feet, a boy and a girl. She held an open book in her hands as if this were story time.

Ella could remember so many hours passed curled up next to her mom as Katie read aloud from a wide array of books. Ella's love of reading had come from her mom as her dad had never been interested in anything but the financial section of the paper.

Honestly, Ella hadn't even registered the fact that he'd appreciated his wife's devotion to reading and creativity. In some ways, he'd been like a ghost in their house—appearing for an occasional dinner or event but then gone again, back to the bank that had taken up so much of his time and energy.

And after her mom died, her father had seemed to vanish into himself, withdrawing to let Ella and Finn fend for themselves amid their own heartbreak.

"You're nothing like her," Anna said as if she had a personal relationship with the statue. As if that heavy piece of metal could truly embody Katie's goodness.

"I know," Ella agreed, because what was the point of arguing? "Congrats on your award. Your dad is super-proud."

"It's not a big deal other than beating Mariah." Anna's cherubic little mouth thinned, which was a surprise. Ella would have expected the girl, who seemed to brim with self-confidence, to enjoy the praise, half-hearted as it was. "Do you know any women like your mom?"

Ella blinked. "Like her how?"

"You know, kind, pretty and nice." Anna kicked the toe of her sandal against the base of the statue. "Single."

"Single, huh? Aren't you a little young to think about dating?"

"It's for my dad," Anna blurted as if Ella was the dimmest bulb in the drawer. "He needs a new wife, and he's bad at picking girlfriends."

And wives, Ella thought, based on what she knew about his ex and the way that woman had left.

"You think he needs someone like my mom?" Her heart pinched at the thought. Any man would be lucky to have a woman like Katie Samuelson at his side. Ella's father certainly had been. "She was a great mom, too."

"I have a mom," Anna said, sounding both defensive and resigned.

A mom who'd walked out as her daughter finished battling cancer. No gold stars there.

Ella's gaze snagged on a flicker of color above the statue. A small butterfly with bright yellow wings landed on the top of her mother's head, and tears stung the back of Ella's eyes.

Shortly after her mom's accident, Ella had been crying in the tree house in their backyard when a butterfly had landed on her arm. It had been late September, the air too cool for the delicate creature, but it was there just the same. Even angry and grieving, Ella had taken it as a sign.

From that moment forward, butterflies meant something more to her, especially when they appeared at unlikely or serendipitous times.

Like right now.

Maybe she was grasping for meaning, but she took the butterfly as a sign from her mom. An unwanted sign based on how she interpreted it, but one she wouldn't ignore.

"I'll help you," she said before she thought better of it.

Anna followed her gaze to the butterfly, which fluttered off to inspect a nearby flower. "Help me do what?" the girl asked slowly.

"Find someone for your dad." Ella let out a long breath as she let the idea of what she was offering wash over her.

This would be good, she told herself. She was leaving Starlight at the end of the summer but helping Josh and Anna Johnson would be a final goodbye to her mother.

A way to connect with Katie's memory and the life her mom would have wanted for Ella. She couldn't be the kind of sweet, nurturing spirit her mom was, but she could help this abandoned girl find someone to fill that role. And then maybe Ella could return to her normal life without being plagued by regrets about how much she refused to give of her heart to anyone.

And how disappointed her mom would be in who Ella had become.

Anna took a step forward. "Why?"

"Because your dad is, indeed, pathetic at choosing women, and I'm a great judge of character." She inclined her head toward the statue. "I had her as a role model, and she'd want me to do this before I leave town again."

Okay, Ella had no idea why she felt the need to get buy-in from an eight-year-old kid. She could find Josh a woman on her own, but she also knew that Anna was the type of daughter who could make things easier or harder in the process.

Ella voted for easier.

Apparently, the girl did, too. She spit on the center of her palm and then thrust out her hand.

"I'm not shaking that," Ella said with a mock shudder. "Gross."

Anna rolled her eyes and wiped her hand on her pink dress, then held it out again. "Fine, but even if we shake without spit, it's a deal. You can't break it."

"Fine." Ella took the girl's hand, surprised by the way the warmth and softness of it ricocheted through her. She quickly drew back. "It's a deal. Operation Dad Date is officially underway."

Chapter Two

Josh drove Anna out to the Tall Pines Camp on Monday morning. He glanced in the rearview mirror as he turned onto the camp's winding driveway.

"You haven't stopped smiling since the art festival," he said to his daughter's reflection. "You must be very proud of that award."

"Sure," Anna agreed as she continued to gaze out the truck's window. "It was fine."

"*Fine* doesn't put that sparkle in your eye," Josh observed. He was happy to see the return of some of his girl's usual effervescence.

His daughter seemed preternaturally capable of retaining her self-assurance and positivity no matter what life threw at her. Cancer—she beat it with a smile on her face. Mom leaves town—she didn't let it get her down. Okay, that was an exaggeration. Of course Anna had been upset and confused when Jenn took off, but his daughter made the best of her circumstances.

His ex-wife only saw Anna a couple of times a year, but Anna regularly told him that their FaceTime conversations and the occasional gifts Jenn sent were fine. She was fine.

Even the therapist they'd gone to in the wake of the divorce had deemed her fine.

Lately she hadn't seemed that way, and he couldn't help but wonder if his kid had been fooling them all by appearing so capable of coping.

He didn't want to believe that because it would mean not only had he failed to keep his family together and make a success of his marriage, but he'd let down the person most important to him in the world.

So this return to her bubbly, boisterous energy was like a balm to his heart. He only hoped it would last. "Are you excited about the start of day camp?"

"Yeah," she answered, pulling a notebook from her backpack. "Do you like blond hair or dark?" she asked.

"Both," he answered slowly as his mind whirled to figure out where the question came from. "I like your hair color best of all."

She scribbled something in the notebook. "Do you like tall people or short?"

He frowned. "I don't have an opinion on height."

"Do you like the smell of vanilla or flowers better?"

"I like the way you smell after a bath."

"Daddy." She jabbed the pencil she held in his direction. "I'm serious. This is for real."

"Vanilla. Why do I feel like I'm taking a quiz and failing? What's the deal, Anna-banana?"

"I just want to know. It's important."

"Okay," he agreed because that was easier than arguing. He loved his daughter with his whole heart, but sometimes he could use his entire brain and still feel like he didn't understand her. He shuddered to think how things would go when she got to her teenage years.

"Waffles or pancakes?"

"That's simple. Blueberry pancakes."

She wrote something else, then shut the notebook and shoved it into her backpack as he took a spot near the far end of the parking lot. He was doing some construction work for Rob and Kayla Jansen, who owned Tall Pines, while Anna was attending a few of the two-week summer sessions. They were paying him a decent hourly rate plus comping her enrollment.

The work was a bit of a departure for Josh at this point. He'd struggled mightily to find his professional footing after his divorce but then bought an abandoned lumber mill in town and successfully renovated and rebranded it into a multiuse space with restaurants and retail shops.

Dennison Mill was wildly successful by all accounts and currently managed by his sister-in-law, Mara. Josh's business had taken off after the mill, and he was working with local developers on several other commercial projects. He'd even had a big-name conglomerate out of California reach out about a partnership.

But as he did each summer since his divorce, he made his best effort to scale back his hours and responsibilities while Anna had her break. Taking the job at the camp was a win-win as it would allow him to stay busy and have the same hours off as his daughter.

"You're going to have the best summer ever," he said as he unbuckled his seat belt and turned to look at her.

She gave him a bright and blatantly mischievous smile. "You, too, Daddy," she said and scrambled out of the car.

"No running in the parking lot," he shouted as he hurried to catch up with her. She'd been his greatest joy and a bundle of energy since the moment she was born.

He waved to several of the parents doing drop-off duty and sidestepped a couple of the more flirtatious moms. He knew it was harmless. He was safe in the dad zone. Just one of the gang, but a single dad was still enough of a rarity in a town like Starlight that his situation held a certain appeal.

He'd made friends with another single dad, Carson Campbell, but he was now off the market and planning a wedding to a pretty redhead who lived on the mountain.

Josh greeted Mara and her daughter, Evie, Anna's best friend, before Anna gave him a quick hug, then shooed him away while she lined up with the other campers.

"Eight going on eighteen," he muttered to Mara.

She grinned in response. "That girl is going to rule the world one day. I hope Evie will be her right-hand woman."

Mara's daughter was the polar opposite of Anna's personality, but they'd been fast friends since the moment they met in kindergarten.

Mara had been one of the few single moms who didn't seem to have designs on Josh, although he'd been shocked when she'd fallen for his sarcastic, temperamental brother, Parker. Now he couldn't imagine a better couple.

A shimmer of wistfulness trickled over him. It wasn't as if he'd expected his marriage to fall apart. He guessed he'd welcome a second chance at love into his life again, but he'd had no luck on the dating scene and had all but given up.

His life was whole enough with Anna and his company and his friends in the community.

Romance was overrated, anyway.

He and Mara briefly discussed a project at the mill that needed his attention, then he grabbed his tool belt from his truck and headed for one of the cabins on the far end of the lake that sat in the middle of the property.

In addition to sessions for kids during the week, the camp hosted weddings as well as family reunions and corporate events during spring, summer and fall. In fact, his friend Carson and his fiancée, Tessa, were getting married at Tall Pines at the end of the summer.

Josh was also doing some work to update one of the bigger barns on the property so it could be used as the main reception space instead of the camp's mess hall. That would allow brides or other renters to decorate earlier the week of their event and not have to deal with young campers disturbing anything.

He breathed in the fresh mountain air and smiled as the sound of children laughing followed him down the path. Anna was among those happy kids. Maybe he'd imagined the recent flatness of her mood. Maybe he'd been projecting his own vague melancholy.

A fish jumped near the lake's center, sending ripples across the previously still water, and Josh mentally ticked off his blessings. They were ample, and he reminded himself to focus on gratitude instead of lack.

He'd been in a dark place during Anna's treatment and his divorce, but he'd turned his life around. So what if he was alone while his brother and most of their friends in town had found love? When would he find the time for dating? Between dad duties and work, his days were packed full.

The nights felt empty, but he could deal with empty for himself as long as Anna was happy.

As he drew closer to the cabin where he was going to begin working, he heard the sound of singing. Bad singing. A cat yowling from its tail being slammed in a door bad.

No one should be over in this part of the property. Kayla had confirmed they wouldn't be booking the cabins until Josh had completed work on each of them. He was redoing the front porches that overlooked the lake. They were original to the construction and years of exposure to the elements had rotted the boards in many places.

He wanted to plug his ears as whoever was inside the cabin got to the chorus of the classic Journey song. She might not stop believing, but he sure wished she'd stop singing.

He called out a greeting as he entered, only to stop short at the sight of Ella Samuelson on her hands and knees in the cozy kitchen area, scrubbing the polished oak floor. Her back end was lifted in the air and her hips shimmied to and fro as she wiped along with the beat, continuing to sing at the top of her lungs.

Josh felt a grin spread across his face.

Clearly she had earbuds in, and he could hear a bit of the music escaping in the otherwise silent cabin. God, she had a horrible voice. Somehow that made it all the more charming, which wasn't something he associated with this woman.

Sarcasm and annoyance were far closer to their normal interactions.

Part of him wanted to sit back and enjoy the performance. There was no doubt Ella was a gorgeous woman with her caramel-colored hair and vivid blue eyes. He would have needed to be dead not to notice that she also had a killer figure. Out of a mixture of respect and self-preservation, he'd done his best not to focus on that during their charged interactions.

He considered himself a mild-mannered guy. His ex-wife would have used the term *weak*, but he didn't really care. Yet, there was something about Ella that pushed buttons in him he hadn't previously realized he possessed.

But the usual buttons weren't being pushed as he watched her. It was his body's reaction to those hips and the obvious fun she was having with something as simple as wiping down a floor that spurred him forward.

"Earth to Ella," he yelled, stomping his feet as he walked toward her.

She stilled and glanced over her shoulder like she'd either heard something or felt the vibration from his boots on the wood. As soon as her gaze snagged on him, she yelped and turned, flinging the rag at him as if in self-defense.

She yanked the earbuds out of her ears and scrambled to her feet. "What in heaven's name is wrong

with you?" she demanded. "You are always sneak-
ing up on me."

"Sorry," he said, folding his hands. "I called out
a greeting but you were too busy trying to scare
away woodland creatures with that caterwauling to
hear me."

"Too bad I didn't scare you away." She stalked
forward to press a button on her phone that silenced
the music coming from the earbuds.

"What are you doing in this cabin?"

"My job." Her tone sounded like a challenge.

"No one is staying here right now."

"Which is why I'm deep-cleaning these cabins,"
she retorted.

"You have a job cleaning cabins?"

Her eyes narrowed. "I have a lot of jobs. It's called
making a living. Perhaps you've heard of it?"

"Why is it that none of the jobs you do involve
nursing? I've heard you're a gifted medical professional."

"I took a sabbatical. It happens."

"You've been back in Starlight way longer than
most sabbaticals last."

"Thanks for noticing. I hadn't realized that."

Josh wasn't surprised by her sarcasm. He liked
the sarcasm. He liked sparring with her. It was the
one time he didn't feel the need to be amiable Josh
Johnson, everybody's friend and helpmate. That role
came naturally to him, but it was a bit of relief to
shrug off the expectations now and again.

"What's your idea of a perfect date?" Ella asked, the change in topic so sudden it made his head spin.

He studied her as the question pinged through his mind, and he discovered with a surprise that his answer wouldn't be what he'd expected.

Several strands of shiny hair had escaped the knot at the back of her head, and her face was flushed with color, whether from embarrassment at being caught singing or the heat that sparked between them, Josh didn't know.

But he very much wanted to because at the moment, any perfect date he imagined involved this woman, which could not end well for either of them.

"I guess a nice dinner and good conversation."

"Basic," she muttered.

He rubbed a hand along the back of his neck and willed away the heat he could feel rising in his cheeks. "There's nothing wrong with basic, and why do you care? Anna was asking me weird questions earlier. What's the deal, Ella?"

She snagged her plump lower lip with her teeth, and awareness zinged through him. If she was trying to distract him, she'd picked a perfect way.

"I'm going to help you find a wife."

Josh blinked. "Come again?"

Her small hands tightened around the rag and her gaze dropped to the floor like she'd revealed too much. "Or a girlfriend," she added. "A match. I'm going to help match you."

"I'm not looking for a girlfriend, and I don't need your help."

She looked at him again with narrowed eyes. "You need help, Josh. You have zero game when it comes to the ladies."

"I have game," he argued, snagging his thumbs in his tool belt.

"You're hot and single and a great dad, which goes a long way. But it's not enough."

"I could get a girlfriend if I wanted one. Wait. You think I'm hot?"

"Don't fish for compliments," she said with an exaggerated eye roll. "My opinion isn't important. When was the last time you went on a date with someone Anna would like?"

Ella's opinion suddenly felt like the only one that mattered, but he shook off the thought. "Anna liked…" Josh searched for a name. He'd gone on so few real dates since his divorce, and he could barely remember anyone who stood out to him. He certainly hadn't introduced her to any of the women he'd dated.

"When was the last time you connected with a woman?"

Ella's tone was gentle, which grated on his nerves for some reason. He'd spent too many years as a child feeling weak and pitiful to take anyone's pity as an adult.

"I've connected plenty, and it's none of your business."

She seemed to wince at that. "I promised Anna I'd match you."

"No." He shook his head. "There is no way I believe you and my daughter made that deal or that she'd ask for your help."

"Desperate times."

"I'm not desperate," he ground out.

"I have ideas," she said, ignoring his words. "They involve you wearing something besides flannel or T-shirts with holes in them."

He glanced down at his faded gray shirt and noticed the hole she'd referenced near the hem. "I work construction."

"Not all the time," she countered. "Also, you need a haircut."

"Seriously, Anna is in on this?"

Ella nodded, looking almost apologetic. "I found her talking to the statue of my mom in the town square during the festival. We made a deal. I can't go back on it."

"Why?"

Her blue eyes seemed to soften to the color of the hydrangeas his ex-wife had insisted he plant along their front porch to give the house more curb appeal. The flowers bloomed each year, but the appeal hadn't kept Jenn from leaving. "It would make my mom happy, and I need that before I leave Starlight again."

His breath caught at the vulnerability he heard in her tone. Ella intrigued him enough with her sharp tongue and prickly vibe…this sweeter version of her was almost too much to take.

"Also, you're pathetic," she added just as he started to step toward her.

He stayed where he was, a safe distance from her. "I don't know—"

"You know." She moved forward, close enough that he could smell the citrusy scent of her shampoo or lotion or… Anna hadn't asked him about citrus when she'd given the choice of his favorite smell.

Right now, citrus topped the list.

"And I know," Ella continued, "that you'd do anything to make your kid happy. She needs this. I don't know why or what's going on, but she needs to believe you're happy so she can be happy."

"I am happy," he lied. "Anna is, too."

"Let me help you," she coaxed.

He wanted to walk away because the way his heart pinched at the thought of really putting himself out there scared the hell out of him. But if Ella was right about Anna wanting this—and somehow he believed her without question—he'd do it. He'd do anything for his daughter.

"Fine," he said, "although I'm not changing my wardrobe."

"We'll discuss it later," she said, glancing at her watch. "I need to meet Kayla in the main cabin. She has a few projects for me there."

"You're a nurse," he reminded her.

"I have many skills," she said with a wink.

Josh could only imagine.

"I'll come up with an initial list of potential ladies. Operation Dad Date is a go."

He groaned. "Do not repeat those words."

"Ten-four," she said with a salute and then grabbed her bucket of cleaning supplies and headed out into the morning sun.

Leaving him to work on the porch in peace, fantasizing about Ella's potential repertoire of skills with far more interest than he should give her.

Chapter Three

Ella picked up the pepper grinder from the counter of her friend Tessa Reynolds's kitchen and held it over the pan of simmering chicken that sat on the stove.

"It's not a terrible idea," she said, glancing over her shoulder to the three women staring at her from the other side of the island.

"The worst," Madison Maurer confirmed, then stepped forward and yanked the pepper mill from Ella's hands. "Also, one more turn on this and you'll ruin the sauce. Have you learned nothing from these months of lessons? You need a delicate touch with spices."

"Pepper isn't a spice," Ella said with a frown.

"Garlic is a spice. Nutmeg is a spice. Pepper is just...
pepper."

"A dried condiment," Tessa added. "Like salt."

Madison, who was an unbelievably talented chef,
looked horrified. "Salt is a seasoning. Pepper is tech-
nically a spice. And I give up." She placed the grinder
on the far end of the counter out of reach. "You people are hopeless."

"I'm learning," Cory Shaeffer offered. "Last week
I made pork chops and they were edible."

"Quite an accomplishment," Madison muttered.
"Lord save me from friends who can't cook."

Ella chuckled at Madison's familiar frustration.
Cory, now married to Jordan Shaeffer, who owned
Trophy Room, the bar and restaurant where Madison
ran the kitchen, had been the one to bring the four
friends together nearly a year and a half earlier when
she moved to Starlight and wanted to make friends.

They'd started the Chop It Like It's Hot cooking
club and had quickly formed a bond that went well
beyond the regular meetings.

Ella had never been much of a joiner and hadn't
realized she cared about having friends when she'd
returned to her hometown. She'd signed up to learn
to cook to impress a man, a coworker she'd fallen for
on one of her far-flung missions who'd been planning a visit to town.

She'd figured if she could show him that she had
a softer side in addition to her skill as both a nurse
and a drinking buddy, it might actually be worth it

to take a chance on love. As it turned out, he'd been coming to visit to ask her to be the best man at his wedding. The relationship had been a bust but she'd made the best friends of her life in the process, which was worth it.

She was still horrible in the kitchen, though, and didn't see any reason to try that hard. It wasn't as if she was looking to go all domestic anyway.

Maybe Cory and Tessa had chosen that path but settling down wasn't for Ella or Madison. The temperamental chef was even less interested in dating than Ella.

"What's the problem with me trying to find someone for Josh?" She grabbed a spoon from the drawer and took a quick bite of the curry sauce bubbling on the stove. It was perfect thanks to Madison's timely intervention. "He and I came to an agreement yesterday. I can't do any worse than he's done."

"The two of you don't even like each other," Tessa pointed out. "How can you match a man with whom you can barely have a civil conversation? Unless…" Tessa step forward. "Unless all the friction is masking some sexual chemistry that neither of you wants to admit. Maybe you're actually the right match for Josh?"

Before Ella could answer, both Cory and Madison dissolved into fits of laughter.

"That's the most ridiculous thing I've ever heard," Madison said.

Ella grinned as well, although it felt somewhat forced.

Of course, she agreed she and Josh weren't a good match, but somehow she didn't appreciate the enthusiasm behind her friends' reactions to the suggestion. "There's no chemistry," she said, "unless you consider mixing oil and water as chemistry."

"Besides, you hate kids," Madison pointed out. "Especially sick kids."

"I don't hate kids. I was a pediatric nurse. I am a nurse. I just needed a little break from it. I'm going back at the end of the summer, and Anna isn't sick anymore."

When her friends continued to watch her in apparent shock, she knew she'd answered with a bit too much intensity. "I'm not doing it for her or Josh, anyway. This mission is for my mom. I found Anna talking to my mother's statue in the park. It was the first time I'd visited it."

"What does that mean?" Tessa tucked a lock of auburn hair behind one ear. "Did she come to you in a vision?"

If someone less earnest had asked the question, Ella would have thought they were making fun of her, but it was clear Tessa was both serious and respectful.

"Not exactly a vision." Ella felt embarrassed that she'd even mentioned it. Her mom had been gone for nearly two decades. And she didn't believe in visions.

But she did believe in butterflies as a sign. "I know it's what I'm supposed to do before I leave Starlight."

To her surprise, no one argued. It was as if the fact that she was doing this to honor her late mother changed everything.

"Who do you have in mind?" Cory asked. "Between the four of us, we know lots of people in town. The right woman is out there."

"Are you sure the right woman isn't in here?" Madison asked as she pulled plates from the cabinet.

"You all agreed that Josh and I would be a terrible match," Ella reminded her.

Madison gave her a curious look. "But what do you think?"

"I think I'm leaving town at the end of the summer, and I'm not getting involved with a single dad."

"Okay," Madison agreed, although it was clear she wasn't convinced. "For the record, I think it's a better idea than you leaving town."

"Exactly." Tessa nodded. "You know there's a nursing shortage. I read about it in the paper the other day. They're doing sign-on bonuses at the hospital. Local doctors' offices are recruiting from out of state. You could help people here."

"I can't stay in Starlight."

"Why?" Cory asked. "There's no rule against it."

"I don't belong in this town and can't make it work. I've been here too long as it is. I don't know how much longer my dad and I can tiptoe around each other without one of us losing it. I don't care that

Finn is all family-first now. This town isn't where I was meant to be."

"You keep saying that." Tessa grabbed one of the plates that Madison had piled with the savory chicken and sauce mixture. "But I don't agree."

"That's because you always see the good in people." Ella grabbed her wineglass from the counter and drained it. "You should give my dad a call. He could tell you the reasons I don't belong here. He can list every one of my faults like he has them on a detailed list in his planner. For all I know, he does."

"I think you should talk to him," Tessa said after an uncomfortably long beat of silence.

Ella hated the feeling of betrayal that speared through her. "You three have talked about this? About my relationship with my dad or the lack of one?" She placed her fork on the plate, suddenly unable to stomach even one bite.

Her life was a bit of a hot mess. She hadn't done much to change that since returning to Starlight but hated the idea that her friends were talking about her and possibly feeling sorry for her. The poor, pathetic woman who'd lost her mom and never really dealt with it.

"We're worried about you," Cory said, and Ella winced.

"I don't need you to worry about me," she told them. "I don't need anyone to worry."

"I wasn't worried," Madison said. "I'm far too self-centered for that. These two…" She hitched her chin at Tessa and Cory. "They're too nice for their own good. Don't let it get to you. You do your thing here and then take off after this summer like we're gravel being tossed up in your rearview mirror."

Ella felt her mouth drop open. "You give a heck of a pep talk," she said with a laugh.

"Thanks," Madison answered. "For the record, I haven't had any of my employees quit in the past three months. Clearly I'm doing something right as a boss, and I should probably make counseling my side hustle."

Ella glanced at Cory, who choked out a laugh. When she'd first come to town, Madison was on the brink of being fired at Trophy Room because she was such a demanding boss.

Cory, who was waitressing at the bar at the time, had been the one to help gentle the acerbic chef. But the influence only went so far.

"Please be on the lookout for women who might be a good fit for Josh." The more Ella thought about it, the more committed she was to make this project a success before she left town.

Their situations were different, but if she could save Anna from the fate of feeling like an abandoned daughter, that would be the right way to start her new chapter.

Her friends agreed and immediately began throwing out names. As they discussed women Josh might like, Ella did her best to ignore the uncomfortable tightening in her stomach.

He wasn't for her. She knew it. He knew it. Even her friends understood it. She'd help Josh and Anna then get on with her life. It would be best for everyone.

As Josh worked outside on one of the cabins the following morning, replacing a rotting deck, he glanced up from his work to see Ella striding toward him. She waved a piece of paper as she approached.

"Who's your favorite matchmaker?" she called out.

For a moment, he couldn't answer, distracted by the fitted T-shirt and leggings she wore. He did not want to notice how attractive Ella Samuelson was.

There was no denying it, but until recently, her beauty hadn't registered for him the same way it did now.

"Stop staring at me like a pervy gym teacher," she commanded.

Josh immediately looked away as he felt his face heat. Why was he always blushing in front of her like some sort of infatuated schoolboy? "I'm not a pervy gym teacher."

"It was a joke, Johnson. I know I'm not your type."

His gaze caught on hers. It had been two days since she'd told him about her arrangement with Anna. Somehow he'd expected to receive a text or instructions on setting up an online dating profile or something to let him know how this was going to go.

He still couldn't quite believe he'd agreed to it and

hadn't been able to bring himself to ask his daughter why she felt it necessary to play matchmaker for him. Her mood had stayed so bright, which he wanted to attribute to summer vacation and having fun with her friends at camp. But the thought that she worried about his happiness weighed on him.

He'd tried to hide both his sadness and lingering worry after the divorce. The doctors seemed confident in her future health, and Josh knew he should trust the experts. He did trust them.

He didn't want her to think he was upset about this little matchmaking deal. If it meant something to Anna, he'd do it.

He placed the sander on the sawhorse and moved toward Ella. He'd set up his work area under a canopy of pine trees to take advantage of the cooler temperatures in the shade.

Ella stood a few feet away, bathed in light. Her hair glimmered in the golden glow as if the sun cradled her. Josh craved that warmth but stayed under the protection of the trees. Like the shade was enough to keep him from wanting her.

"I'm guessing the name of my perfect woman is on that list," he said with more enthusiasm than he felt.

A small line formed between Ella's brows although her smile remained firmly in place. "We have several with a lot of potential."

"Not all of them have potential?"

"They're nice women. Maybe not all of them are

perfect for you. You need a practice date or two," she explained, which made no sense to him.

Obviously, confusion was written on his face because she continued, "We're not going to start with the one I think is the best fit."

"Why?" He shook his head. "I don't have the time or energy to go on any lousy dates, Ella."

"What if you start with the one who's perfect and then mess it up? When was the last time you took a woman out on a date?"

He inclined his head. "It's been a minute but that doesn't mean I don't still have game when it comes to the ladies."

She laughed, then tried and failed to cover it up with a cough.

"What is that reaction supposed to mean?"

"To be honest," she answered with a grimace, "I can't imagine you had game to start. Trust me. You need to know how to interact with women as more than just their dad pal."

"Are you talking cheesy pickup lines? Because that's going to be a hard pass."

She shook her head and moved closer until they were standing toe-to-toe, together under the cool protection of the trees with the fresh scent of pine enveloping them. But Ella brought the light with her, and even more so, the heat. It radiated between them like flames licking at his skin.

"We need to work on you being somebody besides Josh Johnson, everybody's favorite single dad."

"The guy everybody feels sorry for," he muttered. "The guy whose daughter had cancer and his wife left him and he practically lost his house trying to start a business until his brother came and rescued him."

He heard more than saw Ella suck in a breath. "People don't think exactly that about you."

"I know what they think about me." He leaned in. "And they're wrong. Maybe I've had my hands too full to make dating a priority, but that doesn't mean I don't remember what it's like to fill them with a beautiful woman."

Yes, there was something about Ella that made him want to shuck off his easygoing manner. He wanted to put her on edge the way he was constantly discombobulated when she was nearby.

"Do you think the fact that a man knows how to make the best homemade chocolate chip cookies you'll ever taste means he can't woo a potential date? I'll have you know that despite my ability to sing the soundtrack from every princess movie made, I can still kiss a woman so thoroughly she tingles all the way to her toes."

He might be laying it on a little thick. There was a chance he'd never made anyone's toes tingle. But he wanted to kiss Ella that way.

Her gaze held his like a promise. "I didn't say that," she said.

It was a half-hearted argument at best. "You say I need practice." He lifted his hands to cup her face, her skin as soft underneath his calloused palms as he'd imagined it would be. "Let's start practicing now."

Before she could argue, he leaned in and kissed her.

Chapter Four

Ella hadn't expected the kiss, but she wasn't going to lie and claim she didn't want it. She'd thought about kissing Josh but chalked that up to his full mouth and the way he smelled like leather and spice as if he were a cozy chair she wanted to curl up in.

But as his tongue traced the seam of her lips before melding with hers, it was Ella's toes that were curling. Josh Johnson kissed her like he already knew exactly what she wanted. He was firm but not too demanding and seemed willing to take his time and savor her.

The last time Ella had been with a man was back in her traveling days. Everything moved quicker then, furtive and fast because they never knew when they'd be interrupted.

She'd gotten used to that pace. It felt normal. Like it was fine to get to and through the main event without much extra fanfare.

She'd forgotten how amazing simply kissing someone could be. Had it ever been this amazing?

"Relax, Samuelson," he whispered against her mouth, then nipped at the corner of it. "I can hear you thinking. We don't have to think right now. This is practice."

Ella breathed out a little sigh that quickly turned into a moan of pleasure. She didn't think it was possible to turn off her brain, but somehow Josh's words enabled her to do just that.

At the heart of the array of emotions she felt at the moment was a sense of safety. She trusted Josh in a way she couldn't explain and preferred not to consider because of what it might mean. So she just allowed herself to be swept away by the kiss.

By the time he finally pulled away, she'd gone well past tingling. Her body felt like it was on fire. The flames of desire licked at her very core. This man was going to be dangerous for more reasons than Ella had even anticipated.

"How'd I do?" His playful smirk told her he knew exactly how he'd done.

"Passable," she said, smoothing a hand through her hair.

He chuckled at that. "I guess I'll have to work at it some more," he said and leaned in again.

Ella jumped back. "Not with me, buster."

He made a show of looking around. "Did my great-aunt Gert just show up? I haven't had somebody call me buster since the days when Parker and I used to steal butterscotch candies from the bowl on her dining room table. I must have really affected you." He looked so boyishly pleased with himself that Ella couldn't help wanting to smile.

"Well, at least we don't have to work on your confidence," she said with mock relief. "It was a concern."

His features went serious. "It's a legitimate one," he told her, and his willingness to be vulnerable was as much of a shock as the kiss. "I don't want to be seen as the pathetic single dad who needs help finding a date."

"Kiss a few ladies like..." She waved a hand between them. "...like you just kissed me, and no one will think you're pathetic. In fact, I'm half tempted to install you in a kissing booth for the next town festival. We could check out potential matches and raise money for a good cause at the same time."

He looked horrified. "No, thank you. I'll start with your list."

Right. She glanced down at the piece of paper still held between her fingers. She very much wanted to crumple it up and toss it in the trash along with her list of reasons why getting involved with Josh was a bad idea.

"Do you know Kristen Shumaker?"

"She's one of the new teachers at the elementary school, right?"

Ella nodded. "Fifth grade. Moved to town over the summer for the job. She'd been engaged but it ended so she wanted a change of scenery and came to Starlight. She's outdoorsy. Likes mountain biking and has a dog. Not a little fancy one either. A yellow Lab. Mustard."

He inclined his head. "Do you have her social security number in your notes? How did you get so much detail? Tell me you aren't interrogating unsuspecting single women in town."

"Of course not." She inched closer but stayed far enough away that she wouldn't be tempted to pull him to her and plaster herself against him. "I asked Mara and her aunt Nanci to find out her background."

Josh's sister-in-law, Mara, was an extremely talented baker and worked with her aunt at the two locations of the coffee shop Nanci owned. Starlight being a small town, Main Street Perk also functioned as the local bakery and an ice cream shop in the afternoon. Everyone in town came through the stores at one point or another, and Nanci liked to get to know the locals.

"Does Mara know why you wanted the information?"

Ella rolled her eyes. "Oh, sure. I told her I'm trying to get her brother-in-law sexed up."

"That sounds awful," he muttered.

"Sex?"

He dragged a hand through his thick hair and looked out toward the lake. The water appeared so inviting, although it was still early enough in the day that it would be a bit chilly to take a dip. She could hear noise from the campers echo across the water. She'd seen the kids with their counselors on her way to the cabin. They were headed toward the archery range situated in a meadow on the other side of the lake.

"Sex sounds great. The fact that I need someone to help me get it is a problem."

"You could have sex," she assured him. "You want love."

"I don't…" He cringed. "I don't know what I want. It's been a while since I've let myself consider needing anything for myself. Now that this is getting real, I think I should handle my dating life on my own."

"I'm already invested," Ella told him, trying to expunge the sudden, unwelcome image of a naked Josh from her mind. It had been much more manageable when she'd relegated him to the dad friend zone, like so many other people in town.

"Maybe I should have sex with somebody. Anybody. Like you said."

Ella swallowed the protest that bubbled up in her throat. "I didn't say anything about you having random sex."

"But is it a good idea? Test out the waters before another serious relationship?"

Her mind raced at the implications of what he was telling her. "Have you been with a woman since your divorce?"

How had a simple arrangement with a young girl turned into something that felt way more meaningful than she wanted it to?

"I've had a lot going on," he said finally. "Dating hasn't really been on my radar and casual hookups aren't my thing. I don't even want to make them my thing, unless you think I should?"

Yes, I do, Ella thought. *With me. Perhaps right now in an empty cabin.* Her body hummed to life once again. If he'd been that good at kissing, she could only imagine how great all the other stuff would be.

"No," she blurted, apparently with more force than she meant by the way he stared. "I mean, if that's what you want, then go for it, but I don't think it's necessary. What I have in mind for you is practice dating, not necessarily practice sex."

"That's a good point."

He seemed to consider her words. "Things are rarely as uncomplicated as they seem. Who knows if falling in love again is a real possibility. Although I also don't know if dating a teacher at school is a great idea. At least not as my practice girlfriend. What if things go badly and then Anna has her for a teacher? I've heard she's a good teacher. Fifth grade is an important year."

"Nicole Martin," Ella suggested.

"The real estate agent?"

"Single mom. Likes CrossFit and skinny vanilla lattes."

"I've thought about trying CrossFit," Josh said. "I could be in a little bit better shape." He did a couple of poses, flexing his muscles in an exaggerated way. "Can you see me tossing around a tire or two?"

Although Ella knew he was joking, her mouth went dry. She was going to need to get this guy matched quickly and maybe find a partner for practice sex on her own so that she didn't get so worked up every time she was in Josh's presence. There was no reason for that.

"We'll start with Nicole. According to Nanci, she comes into the coffee shop every Tuesday and Thursday after her class at the new studio downtown."

He nodded, although he looked dubious. "So I'm signing up for a CrossFit class?"

"It's all the rage," Ella told him. "You'll have fun."

"You should go with me."

She shook her head. "I'd rather cover myself in honey and let a swarm of killer bees have at me."

"You are my wingwoman."

"I came up with her name."

"But what if it's terrible? What if we don't hit it off? What if I need help with my moves?"

"You don't need help. Trust me. You've got the toe-tingling thing down to a science."

He flashed a satisfied smile. "I still want you to come. If you're leaving at the end of the summer, we don't have a lot of time. You promised Anna this would work. Your mother would want you to help."

Ella snorted. "Are you seriously using my late mother's memory to finagle me into an exercise class I don't want to do?"

"I am." He nodded. "One hundred percent."

"Fine," she relented. "I'll be there, but if I tell you to make a move, you have to make it."

"Okay," he agreed, way too readily. He opened his mouth to say more, then shut it again but continued to stare at her.

Ella threw up her hands. "What?"

"I'm wondering if you might want to practice a little more. Make sure I'm ready for meeting a potential girlfriend."

"Not interested," she lied. "I'll see you at the gym tomorrow." It took every ounce of willpower she possessed to turn and walk down the path toward the cabin she was painting on the far end of the lake.

"Hell no." Parker Johnson, Josh's older brother by two years, held up his hands, palms forward, as he shook his head. "You can't let Ella match you. That's like letting Lucifer lead you to the gates of heaven."

Finn Samuelson paused with a beer halfway to his mouth. "Did you just compare my sister to the devil?"

"It was an example," Carson Campbell clarified and patted Parker on the shoulder. "A really awful one that you should never use again."

Josh shook his head. "Ella is not Lucifer."

He sat at one of the high-top tables near the front of Trophy Room with Parker, Finn and Carson. Parker and Finn had been childhood friends, along with the town's sheriff, Nick Dunlap. Nick was currently on duty so not with them to watch the Mariners game at the popular local bar.

Anna was spending the night at Parker and Mara's house that night. She and Evie were practicing for the camp talent show, which would take place at the end of their two-week session. The two girls were creating a dance routine and divided their time between Josh's and Parker's for practice. Until his brother had returned to town, Josh hadn't left Anna's side other than when he went to work.

Now he realized he'd been holding on to her too tightly. He wanted to protect her and keep her safe from any real or imagined danger and felt a constant sense of dread that something like cancer could threaten her again and he'd have no control over it.

He appreciated reconnecting with Parker and having his brother's friends see him as something more than an annoying tagalong nuisance. He and his brother had dealt with their father's temper in very different ways when they were younger. Parker had tried to make himself as hard-nosed as their dad had been, allowing everyone to believe he didn't care about anyone or anything.

Josh had cared too much. He'd believed that by being meek and compliant he could keep himself out of his dad's crosshairs when things went bad. Instead, his need for love and approval had made him more of a target, a lesson he hadn't learned until his sophomore year of high school when a sudden heart attack had killed Mac Johnson and ended the nightmare of Josh's childhood.

Despite all the bad memories this town held, he'd never dreamed of leaving Starlight. It was his home, although life in the small town was far from perfect. Several of the guys he'd grown up with had either moved away or had grown distant since his divorce. When Anna had been going through treatment, a few of the kids in her class had made her feel even worse about the cancer by acting like it was catching.

Evie, who'd been new to the school at that time, had been the one to befriend his daughter and keep her spirits and confidence from flagging.

Josh sometimes felt like he was the contagious one, as if people kept him at arm's length because of what he'd been through. Like his hard times might rub off on them. But he loved the town and the mountains, and it was the home both he and Anna knew.

"I'd let Ella set me up on a date," Carson offered. "She's got good instincts. Tessa trusts her implicitly." He tipped his head toward Josh. "She's a great judge of character other than the fact that she doesn't like you. That's a bright red flag."

"Everyone likes Josh," Parker said, always the big brother.

"Not Ella." Finn placed his elbows on the table

and leaned forward. "Carson is right. I'd be wary, man. My sister has a warped sense of humor. She might push you into some questionable situations for her own amusement."

Josh's mind returned to the kiss he and Ella had shared outside the cabin at Tall Pines. She'd seemed to like him well enough then. For his part, he'd liked everything about her at that moment.

"We're not exactly best friends," Josh told the table in general, "but she doesn't hate me. We get along fine."

The silence that greeted his words gave a clear message—he was fooling himself. His stomach pitched. His dad used to play mind games with him—making Josh believe he cared only to take sadistic pleasure in crushing his hopes.

Mac had been Starlight's beloved mayor for many years. For all his glad-handing and backslapping in public, his true personality had come out behind closed doors. Street angel, house devil was how Josh's mom had described it.

Parker had managed his dad better than Josh. He'd been the kind of son their father expected—brash, confident, the star of every team he joined.

Josh had played sports because it meant something to his dad, but he'd never had the competitive drive Mac expected. In high school, Josh had found his niche with the drama department kids. He'd built and painted sets for theater productions until his father had forced him to quit because the theater was for sissies.

A commanding physical presence, Josh towered over most kids in his class, so his dad had pushed him toward football. Despite his size and strength, Josh didn't have the inherent aggression to excel on the field.

His father had made him feel like a complete disappointment for having interests of his own.

Was Ella doing the same thing as his father? Setting him up just to make a fool of him?

He didn't want to believe it, but he'd put his faith in enough people who'd let him down to know he couldn't always trust his intuition.

"Maybe she doesn't like me," he admitted, even though it hurt his heart to say the words out loud, "but she offered to help because of some deal she made with Anna." He focused on Finn. "It has something to do with your mom and honoring her memory before Ella leaves town again."

Regret speared through him as soon as he spoke the words. The way Finn's jaw went slack, he knew he'd revealed too much. If Ella hadn't mentioned her thoughts about her mother's memory to her brother, it wasn't Josh's place to share it.

"She told you that?" the buttoned-up banker asked.

Josh nodded.

"That's a different story." Finn looked toward Parker. "She'll take care of him."

"I can take care of myself," Josh protested through

gritted teeth. "Anna wants this, so I'm giving it a try with Ella's help. If it makes my kid happy…"

All three of the men nodded, and Josh felt a small measure of his frustration dissipate. This deal was for Anna. He might not trust or believe in love for himself, but he'd give anything a try for his daughter.

Chapter Five

Ella parked her compact Toyota next to Josh's giant truck the following morning and stepped out at the same time as him.

"Good morning," he said with a wave. "You ready to flip some tires or whatever it is we'll be doing?"

"Take off your shirt," she said as they met at the sidewalk.

"Somebody needs coffee." Josh shook his head. "Also, no thanks on going into class shirtless."

"You have a hole in your sleeve." She reached out a finger and poked at his arm, which was hard as granite. Josh was a mix of contradictions—soft-spoken, consummate dad and complete good guy in the body of a street fighter or defensive lineman, all hard angles and toned deliciousness.

"It's a CrossFit class. No one will care about how I look."

"Nicole will. She's polished, so you can't look…" She grasped for the right word because the adjectives that came to mind were *mouthwatering* and *scrumptious.* Not exactly the message she was trying to convey. "Frumpy," she settled on.

"Who shows up to a class with no shirt on? This isn't the high school locker room. Kind of a cheesy move and that also won't fly for me."

"I have a solution." She reached into her purse and pulled out the emergency kit she kept there. She opened it to reveal a pair of mini scissors. "Sleeveless will work. You'll lose the hole and show off those biceps as well."

He grimaced. "We are well beyond my comfort zone."

"Remember you said you'd take my advice."

"My friends, including your brother, think you might be setting me up to look like a fool."

"Why would I do that?"

"Because you don't like me."

Ella did her best to hide how much it hurt that people she'd known her whole life would think she had it in her to be so devious. Especially her brother. Ella wasn't effusively kind, but she thought of herself as cynical, not mean.

"I'm trying to help you and your daughter," she

said. "Keep the shirt on. Maybe ladies find holes in clothes appealing. You're a project for them. Their love will give you a new lease on life. Don't change a thing." She stepped closer. "But we both know how far an unwillingness to change or grow has gotten you. Let's not pretend otherwise."

To her astonishment, he grabbed the hem of his T-shirt and whipped it off without another word.

She wanted to believe she'd gotten through to him but couldn't help wondering if he was doing this because she needed him matched as much as he did. Her vow to her mother meant something, and Josh seemed to understand that. He was helping her as well, although she wasn't going to come to depend on it.

Ella knew she was the type of woman who could push away any man whom she came to depend on. She might not feel in control of most areas of her life, but that was something she could take to her family's bank.

She also didn't have a lot of time to process Josh's motivations because she was too distracted by his chest. "Please tell me you weren't just born that way," she said as she took the shirt from him. "Because it's so unfair if you don't have to work to look like you could model for a hot contractor calendar."

She expected some teasing retort, but he shrugged and looked vaguely embarrassed. "I have a home gym set up in the basement. After Jenn left and Anna was in recovery, there was a period of time I didn't have much use for being social. But I had some frustrations I needed to deal with, and lifting weights seemed better than drinking myself into a stupor every night when I knew I had to take care of my kid the next day."

"That's admirable." She began to cut the sleeves off his shirt. "Not quite a shock at this point. I'm beginning to think you could show up for dates wearing a potato sack and it wouldn't matter. You are a catch, Johnson."

"My ex-wife didn't think so."

"Stupid."

She finished altering the sleeves and handed the shirt back to him. "Cover yourself, man. The perfection is blinding me."

"Stop it." He put the shirt on again, and Ella admired her handiwork, as well as his toned arms. "You're being silly."

"I've never in my life been accused of being silly." She shoved the extra fabric into her purse and put away the scissors. "Let's go."

They walked toward the new fitness center. It had opened a few months ago as a sort of co-op with yoga, Pilates, some sort of aerobic dance classes plus CrossFit.

"Is this going to be awkward?" Josh asked. "Am I supposed to ask out a woman I barely know in the middle of doing burpees?"

"She knows you're coming," Ella said.

Josh grabbed her arm. "Excuse me?"

"I made sure I ran into Nicole at Main Street Perk

yesterday and told her I had a friend who wanted to ask her out."

"That's embarrassing as hell. Are we back in junior high where I slip her a note and she can check a box if she likes me?"

She took his hand from her arm and tugged him along the sidewalk, ignoring how good his calloused palm felt cradled in hers. "Trust me. You aren't pathetic. She's flattered." Ella squeezed his fingers. "And interested."

"In me?"

"No, in Santa Claus. Yes, you, you big dork. You're the one I'm doing this for."

He looked adorably flabbergasted, like he'd forgotten the purpose of their arrangement. As if the matchmaking scheme was an excuse for the two of them to spend time together.

Ella was not going to admit how much she liked spending time with him.

They got to the gym's entrance, and she forced herself to drop his hand. She wasn't a hand-holder, even with a man she liked romantically. But, gosh, Josh's hand felt good in hers.

As he opened the door, a flash of color caught Ella's attention. She glanced toward one of the flower boxes perched on the building's front windowsill and saw a tiny butterfly flitting from bloom to bloom, which had to be a sign she was doing the right thing.

This had to mean her mother approved. Her resolve bolstered by the tiny creature, she approached the front desk, where she and Josh both paid for a one-day pass.

They joined the other participants, including Nicole Martin, in the biggest room, where various sets of weights and hulking machines were laid out in a configuration that brought to mind images of medieval torture chambers. Nicole smiled at Josh, who made a face in response. Ella imagined someone who'd just been tased would offer a similar expression.

Nicole frowned, then turned her attention back to the bald, tattooed, middle-aged instructor, who was giving the breakdown of the WOD, which apparently stood for workout of the day. It involved a lot of exercises Ella wasn't interested in doing, but she kept that butterfly in the forefront of her mind.

She also pinched Josh under his arm.

He jerked away from her.

"Head in the game, Johnson," she commanded. "Don't scare her off with your weird face before you even talk to her."

"I'm not sure I want to date a woman who willingly subjects herself to that..." he pointed toward the whiteboard on the wall where the class outline was written "...on a regular basis."

"It's going to be fun," Ella lied.

The instructor, whose name was Tin for some unknown reason, told them to break into partners for the hour-long session. Ella instinctively took a step toward Josh, only to realize he was moving in Nicole's direction.

"I'm going for it," he said over his shoulder.

She gave him a thumbs-up that he didn't see, then thought of ducking out quickly before any of the hard stuff started.

The next thing she knew, she was facing Mr. Offkowski, her tenth-grade biology teacher. He had to be well into his sixties, a gentle giant of a man who'd coached JV football as well as taught science.

"My prodigal student is back and ready to get her butt kicked," he said with an almost maniacal chuckle. "You'll be my partner."

Ella gave a sharp shake of her head. "I'm not sure that I—"

"Nonsense. You'll be fine. I'll show you the ropes. I was once a newbie to WODs, but I'm getting back in shape. The wife and I are going on a fortieth anniversary cruise at the end of the summer. I'm sick of being at the pool with my shirt on like I'm a toddler."

He patted his round belly. "I'm looking for six-pack abs. Burpees are going to get me there. With a few mountain climbers thrown in for good measure. What's your why?"

"I don't know what that means."

"You need to know why you're committed to this."

Ella glanced at Josh. He and Nicole were taking turns lifting a kettlebell high in the air. As Ella watched, the woman leaned over and pressed an admiring hand on Josh's bare arm, the way Ella would have liked to.

"It's for my mom," she said softly. She hadn't planned to share such a personal tidbit with her former teacher but she needed the out-loud reminder. "It would make her happy to know I'm stepping out of my comfort zone and trying new things."

"That's a good why. She died, right?"

Ella nodded.

"You want to stay healthy because of her?"

Not exactly, but she didn't correct the assumption. Her throat felt too tight to manage the words. "Can we just start on the exercises?" she asked.

"Let's do this, girl. You were a gifted student, although I had to dress-code you way too much because you couldn't follow the rules. But I know you've got grit."

"You do?" Lately Ella felt as though she was made of more spun sugar than grit. But she followed Mr. Offkowski as he counted out reps.

The class was worse than she'd imagined. Within minutes she was drenched in sweat, and her thigh muscles trembled during the wall sit while Mr. Offkowski detailed his cruise itinerary for her.

She spent the next forty-five minutes trying to ignore the instructor, who shouted out encouraging platitudes like he was reading from a script of cliched motivational quotes, as well as Mr. Offkowski's unending chatter and the fact that she kept hearing Nicole's horsey laugh ring through the gym.

She tried to catch Josh's eye a couple of times and gauge how he was doing, but he refused to hold her gaze for more than a cursory second at a time.

By the time they finished class, Ella was tired,

sore and far more annoyed than she had a right to be. Josh was doing exactly what she wanted. Why did it make her so mad?

Nicole wasn't the type of person Ella would want to hang out with, but she was a single mother, so at least she had experience dealing with kids. Anna would like that.

And she had a killer body, that was undeniable. Josh had to like that very much. Which still left Ella enjoying nothing about the hour other than the thought she could have her favorite doughnut with no guilt thanks to all the calories she'd burned.

She planned to wait for Josh and walk out together but after Tin dismissed the class, he pulled Josh and Nicole aside. Probably to congratulate them on being the unofficial poster couple for ridiculously fit people. He might even include them in some sort of social media campaign to draw in other beautiful people.

It appeared that Josh had been right. He didn't need any sort of practice. For all his talk about bumbling interactions with women, he'd done a bang-up job his first time out of the gate.

Ella quickly grabbed her purse from one of the cubbies and headed toward the bakery. Her work there was done. Now she just wanted the comfort of some fried dough and sprinkles to make herself feel okay.

Josh was relieved to see Ella's small car in the Tall Pines parking lot the following morning when he and Anna arrived. He'd looked for her the previous day, but she never made an appearance.

He'd wanted to tell her what a successful matchmaker she turned out to be, even if it wasn't in the way she planned.

He winced as he grabbed his toolbox from the bed of the truck.

"Why are you walking funny?" Anna asked. "Are your underpants too tight?"

Josh breathed out a laugh. "My underpants fit perfectly fine and thank you for asking. I overdid it at a CrossFit class yesterday."

"What's CrossFit?"

"A form of exercise I will not be engaging in anymore."

"No offense, Daddy, but you're not even good at softball."

"I'm fine at softball. And let's remember that I am a fantastic soccer coach."

"We're little girls. Nobody is trying to make the Olympic team."

As if he needed another reminder of how low the stakes were in his life.

"It doesn't make me care any less," he told her.

She took his hand as they walked. "I know. That's why you're the best."

Moments like this were why his daughter had him wrapped around her little finger. He'd do one million burpees to deserve the love she gave to him so freely.

He checked her in for camp, surprised to see Parker instead of Mara dropping off Evie.

"If your slick big-city friends could see you now," he said as his brother approached.

Parker had been adamant about getting out of their small town and away from the memory of Mac Johnson and his temper.

He'd done it, too, becoming one of Seattle's most successful divorce attorneys. But after falling in love with Mara, Parker had softened. He'd taken over a law practice in Starlight and now happily made his home here. Josh liked to think he'd been right about staying all along.

"You aren't returning my calls," Parker said.

"We saw each other the other night at Trophy Room. I've been busy since then."

"Busy avoiding me." Parker placed a hand on Josh's arm. "The real estate group wants an answer."

"I'm busy."

"This is a huge opportunity, Josh."

A few months ago, a developer out of California had approached him about absorbing Josh's company into their extensive network throughout the western United States.

According to Parker, it was a testament to what Josh had so quickly built in Starlight, and the incentive and benefits package would ensure his and Anna's future.

He didn't want to think about how important good health insurance would be if she needed it. He couldn't let himself go there, but the reality stayed with him always.

Parker had offered to look at the contract and stepped in to help broker the deal when Josh let it slide.

He didn't plan to pass up this opportunity on purpose. It was simply hard to think about success on a larger scale. Anytime he'd gone after something on a more significant level, he'd ended up losing it. Almost losing everything in some cases.

What if that happened again? What if he took a risk, things went sideways and he jeopardized his daughter's security?

The incentives were huge, but the risks were even greater. He'd carved out a decent niche for himself even if sometimes he knew he passed on certain deals because they would push him more than what he wanted.

This deal would be a huge push.

"It's summer break," he said, as if that explained everything. "You know that means Anna is priority number one. I'm not going to make changes until the new school year."

"We can negotiate that," Parker agreed. "But if you don't give them an answer, they'll find somebody else to handle this region. I keep stalling but sooner than later they'll want a final answer, Josh. You know what that answer should be."

Josh stopped at the back of his brother's car. He wanted this conversation ended. "That's easy for you to say. Especially after you gave up the stress and demands of a high-pressure career when you decided to stay in Starlight. But now you want me to—"

"I want you to live up to your potential for once," Parker snapped. "I want you to stop believing the crap Dad said to you and the way he put you down. I want you to know you are better than that. Dennison Mill was supposed to prove it, Josh, but it clearly wasn't enough for you. You need to do more. You need to be more. So do it."

"Now you sound like Dad." Josh massaged a hand along the back of his neck as dissatisfaction rolled through him. Dissatisfaction with himself, which was as familiar as his reflection in the mirror. "I'll give you an answer soon."

A muscle ticked in Parker's jaw. Josh had been watching that tell of frustration on his brother for his whole life.

"It's going to be good," Parker promised him.

But Parker couldn't be certain of that. Nobody could be certain of anything except that Josh wouldn't get hurt if he didn't try. They said goodbye, and he headed for the cabin where Ella was still working on painting. He hoped to catch her unawares once again, singing off-key. The memory of it brightened his mood slightly, but she must have heard his approach because she turned as he entered the cabin.

"I'm busy," she said, which was a bit of a downer of a greeting.

"Do you want to hear about your excellent match-making skills?"

Her hand tightened on the roller, but she didn't face him again. "It was pretty clear things were going well. You can let me know when you're ready to try again but maybe we hit a home run your first time at bat."

"We sure did," he agreed. He could feel the tension radiating from her but still she didn't turn. "For Nicole and Tin," he added.

The paint roller stilled. "What are you talking about? I saw the two of you."

"Apparently, the Realtor and the CrossFit instructor have been crushing on each other since he opened the studio. She brokered the deal for him. But until he felt some sort of threat from me, he was too afraid to do anything. That all changed in the class. So way to go. You made your first successful match. It just didn't involve me."

She turned to him finally. Was he misreading the look of relief that warred with confusion in her deep blue eyes? "You were flirting with her. I was surprised you didn't lift her over your head for a couple of bench presses. Really show off your strength."

"I was helping her attract him."

Ella placed the paint roller in the tray and wiped her hands on a nearby towel. "I don't understand. She told me she was interested in you."

He shrugged. "It wasn't like she actively dislikes

me, but I would have been a sloppy at-bat substitution for the guy she wants to be her main hitter."

"She picked the CrossFit dude over you? Is she stupid?"

It wasn't exactly a compliment but Josh chose to take it as one, especially coming from Ella. "I think she picked him before me. They're cute together. She's a type-A personality and he's a man who gives unironic pep talks about digging deep and loving the burn. She wouldn't be Anna's type. She wasn't my type either."

"Huh." Ella tapped a finger against her chin. "I will need to consider that."

"Plus, I don't ever want to do CrossFit again. That was awful."

"The worst," she said.

He grinned. She wore a denim shirt and olive-colored cutoffs, and her hair was pulled back in a high ponytail with some sort of scarf keeping it out of her face or protecting her from paint splatter. The freckles across the bridge of her nose were an adorable contrast to her creamy skin. If Josh had to describe his perfect woman at that exact moment, it would be Ella.

She grinned at him. "But I ate a doughnut with no guilt, which hasn't happened for years."

"You have doughnut guilt?"

"It's not the worst kind of guilt to have," she countered.

"No, but it's useless when a person looks the way

you do, which is perfect," he told her, unable to say anything else. It was completely true, although he hoped the words didn't reveal too much.

He and Ella had forged a sort of tentative friendship, and he didn't want to put that in jeopardy. It might be new, but his feelings for her were far too precious to risk.

Chapter Six

Ella knew she was nowhere near perfect but appreciated Josh's comment all the same. Almost as much as she secretly gave thanks for the fact that he and Nicole hadn't been a good match.

She told herself it was because she could find someone better for him—just not her. Ella wasn't the right match for Josh. There was a laundry list of reasons she could tick off to support that fact.

He'd do best with a woman who could be virtuous and domestic. Ella had no use for either of those characteristics.

Josh was dedicated to staying in Starlight, and she was leaving, despite her friends wanting her to change her mind.

Anna. That was nonnegotiable. Ella could not—would not—step in as a maternal role model for any child, let alone one who'd dealt with cancer. She could spout all the statistics she wanted on the survival rate from childhood cancer, but the facts didn't matter. When Ella cared about someone or something, she got left behind. So she refused to care about Josh or his daughter.

"I feel like things might have gone better with Nicole if I'd had more practice."

Ella gasped as Josh's hand came around the back of her neck and massaged away the tension she hadn't even realized she was carrying there.

"Practice," she repeated, getting lost in those whiskey-colored eyes.

"Yep." He nipped at the corner of her mouth. "They say it makes perfect, and I'm looking to remake my reputation as a perfectionist."

Ella laughed but it quickly turned into a moan as Josh trailed open-mouthed kisses along her jaw and down her neck. "You have the most beautiful skin," he said against it. "It's easy to believe in perfection with you."

"Did you give Nicole that kind of compliment?" she asked as she tried to keep her attention focused on what should be happening instead of what she wanted to happen. They should be discussing his next potential date. Instead, Ella wanted to rip off the drop cloth she'd placed over the leather sofa that sat against one wall and pull Josh down onto it with her. Only her.

"No," he said as he threaded his hands through her hair. "Only you, Ella. I only talk this way to you. I only kiss this way with you." He claimed her mouth again.

That was exactly what she wanted to hear, and she met him stroke for stroke as the kiss deepened. Her arms encircled his lean waist, and she inched her hands under his T-shirt. She could think of nothing she wanted more than to touch his bare skin.

And nothing she wanted less than the sound of an ATV approaching the cabin. The roar of the motor got louder, then cut off, and Ella wrenched herself away from Josh. Footfalls pounded up the stairs, and Kayla burst through the door.

"Ella, we need you."

She smoothed a hand over her hair as she turned. Would it be obvious what she and Josh had been doing?

Kayla glanced between the two of them before she narrowed her eyes at Ella. "Our regular nurse had a family emergency, and one of the campers had an accident."

Kayla's gaze flicked to Josh.

"Is it Anna?" he demanded, stepping around Ella.

"She wanted Ella to look at it before we got you involved," Kayla said. "You know how she is, Josh. For a little kid, she's adamant."

"She's also my little kid," he countered. "I'll take a look and then we'll get her to the doctor."

Ella placed a hand on his arm. "Take a breath."

"Don't tell me to—"

"Take a breath," she repeated. "Anna needs you to hold it together, whatever is going on."

They followed Kayla into the vibrant sunshine.

"Trust me," Josh grumbled. "I know all about holding it together. I'm the one who held it together when everything fell apart."

Ella knew he was talking about his daughter's battle with cancer and his wife leaving. The ATV was a four-seater model, and she climbed into the back while Josh took the seat next to Kayla in front. As the camp's owner drove, she explained how the accident had happened.

The kids had been on the zip line course, and Anna hadn't pushed the break on one of her approaches and slammed into a counselor, propelling both of them forward into one of the large wood columns that held the apparatus. The counselor was fine, but Anna's wrist had hyperextended in the crash.

"Is she still able to move it?" Ella asked.

Kayla nodded.

Ella could feel Josh's tension. She didn't exactly want to get involved with his daughter when she was hurt. She didn't want to get involved at all. But there was no other choice since she was the only nurse available at the moment.

It took a few minutes to get to the main cabin. "We sent everybody off on a wilderness hike," Kayla explained. "I didn't think anything would happen with Susan gone for a few hours. But it seemed better if there weren't a bunch of scared kids gawking. Evie asked to stay with her, and Anna seemed to want that." She glanced at Josh. "I hope it's okay."

"My kid is hurt," he replied tersely. "Nothing about this is okay."

So much for easygoing Josh. Ella sighed. They entered the cabin, and Kayla led them down the hall toward the room that was outfitted as the nurse's office.

Ella did her best to keep her mind focused on the present moment and not the way her heart pounded at the thought of dealing with an injured child.

This terror was old and familiar. But she thought she'd gotten over the worst of her anxiety. She was going to be leaving Starlight at the end of summer to return to her old job where she'd be dealing with children who had much more serious injuries than a collision at the end of a zip line, life-and-death situations that she couldn't make better.

Anna sat on the exam table with Evie next to her holding her hand. Ella appreciated the tight bond between the girls. She wished she'd had a friend like that growing up.

She wished she could find a way to open up and let the friends she had now support her in that way.

Tears stained Anna's pink cheeks, but she wasn't crying at the moment.

"I'm fine, Daddy," she said immediately.

Ella wasn't sure what to make of the fact that the girl's first inclination was to comfort her father even though she was in obvious pain. She admired Anna's pluck.

"Is it okay if I take a look?" she asked the girl as she went to the sink to wash her hands. "I heard you had an issue with your dismount."

Anna gave her the ghost of a smile, and she expected Josh to chide her for the inappropriate humor at his daughter's expense. When she looked over, he'd gone completely still at the room's doorway, staring at Anna in a way that made Ella understand she wasn't the only one having trouble releasing the past at this moment.

"I'm going to go check on the hikers," Kayla said and quickly disappeared from the room. Evie moved off the table.

"Take a breath, Dad," Ella said to Josh in the tone she reserved for anxious parents. "Everything's going to be okay."

She knew from experience that an exam would go better with a child if their parent wasn't actively freaking out.

But it was difficult to tell if Josh even heard her. His gaze had gone glassy and remained focused on Anna. Her little rosebud mouth had thinned, and Ella knew she was picking up on the tension from her dad.

Parents often experienced symptoms of traumatic stress that manifested in feeling overwhelmed or reliving what happened to the child even when they wanted to avoid it. Ella could imagine that seeing his daughter in pain would trigger a variety of difficult memories for Josh.

"Josh." She said his name with more force. He startled, and then his gaze flicked to hers. "Come into the room and shut the door. I'm not familiar with how this office is set up. While I'm doing the examination, take a look through the drawers and cabinets to find a bandage to wrap her wrist."

She thought he was going to ignore her, but he moved forward. Before he went to the cabinet, he planted a kiss on Anna's forehead and gave her a gentle hug. "You okay, Banana?"

The girl visibly relaxed. "I'm okay, Daddy. It only hurts a little."

"So brave," he whispered.

"Your father makes a terrible assistant." Ella nudged him out of the way. "Doesn't take direction well."

"What can I say? I like to be my own boss." He winked at his daughter and Evie. Ella was relieved to see that he'd snapped out of the worst of his anxiety.

Ella started the examination. She asked the girl some questions and palpated her wrist. It had swelled only slightly, and from what Ella could tell, she'd suffered a minor sprain.

"We have the camper competition at the end of next week," Anna told her as she wrapped the wrist with a compression bandage and a splint. "Me and Evie are part of the Tall Pines Terrors. They're going to need me to win. I won't have to sit on the sidelines, right?"

"You should be fine. Your dad should follow up with the pediatrician, but I think a couple of days of rest and you'll be good as new. Just pay attention when your counselors give you instructions during activities."

"They were taking pictures for the website," Anna explained. "I wanted to make sure that I did something funny when I came in on the zip line so I get my face on the website."

Josh moved forward again. "I'm more concerned with keeping your face and the rest of your body in one piece."

"If you ask Miss Kayla, I bet she'll put you on the website anyway," Evie suggested. "She might even hire you to be one of her photographers."

"Yeah," Anna agreed reluctantly. "I should have just asked. I know you're going to be on the website, Evie. I got the best picture of you. I'll show it to Miss Kayla, and you'll be a star."

"You take all the best pictures." Evie was forever loyal.

Anna grimaced as Ella secured the end of the bandage.

"Who's Daddy's next date with?" she asked Ella. "One of the boys we met this session said his mom is single. They just moved to town. Do you want me to get her number?"

Josh cleared his throat. "First of all, we are dealing with your wrist and not my dating life right now."

He tapped one finger on the top of Anna's head. "And second, I'm standing right here. Why are you asking Ella about my next date instead of me?"

"Because she's in charge," Anna said as if that were obvious.

"She's helping," Josh argued. "She's not in charge. I'm in charge of my life. I'm in charge of your life, too. I'm telling you no more stunts like today."

"I'm helping to screen potential candidates," Ella clarified for both of them but didn't bother to hide the way her mouth twitched with humor.

Anna was a uniquely confident kid. Ella knew it would take a remarkable woman to appreciate that. She'd been a handful as a child and none of the women her father had dated casually after her mom died had seemed to want anything to do with her.

She couldn't blame them. She didn't make it easy on her dad. Or anyone, even herself.

She had a feeling that despite wanting a woman for Josh, Anna would have high standards. Ella could admire the girl's discernment even though she understood at a soul-deep level that she would never live up to it.

That night Josh stood at the open door of Anna's bedroom and watched as she slept.

The day felt like it had taken a few years off his life, although the pediatrician had agreed with Ella's assessment that the wrist was only mildly sprained and Anna would have full use of it within a week.

Josh shouldn't feel any blame for the accident. It could have happened to any of the kids at any time. On occasion, he wondered if Anna's penchant for being the center of attention had intensified after the divorce. It's part of why he hadn't dated. He wanted to make sure his daughter knew she was the most important person in his life.

Of course, she hadn't known at the time of the accident that he'd been kissing and thinking of doing much more with Ella, but that didn't change the fact.

How was he supposed to even consider falling in love again when it would impact the dynamic of their lives on such a profound level?

His cell phone dinged from his bedroom across the hall. He shut Anna's door and went to retrieve it.

He figured it was Parker or his mom checking in. Instead, Ella's number lit up the screen.

Just wanted to see how Anna is feeling.

Warmth infused his heart at the fact that she'd reached out. Stupid heart.

She'd been fantastic with both Anna and Evie during the examination, and he wondered again why she'd taken a break from nursing when she was clearly gifted.

Doc says she'll be good as new in a couple of days. Thanks for your help.

He thought about texting more. Asking her to come over for dinner the following evening. Nothing more than a thank-you between friends.

Because no matter the friction that shimmered between them like sun glinting off rippling water, he'd now come to consider Ella a friend.

She was the kind of friend he preferred because he didn't have to be someone different with her. He could let the mask of affability drop when he felt like it. Plus, he didn't worry about shocking her or sending her running in the other direction to spread the word that Anna's dad wasn't the good-natured nice guy they all assumed him to be.

His childhood had taught him about getting along and putting on a happy face to make people feel comfortable, even when it was the last thing he truly felt.

Before he could tap out the words, another message from her appeared on the screen.

Checked out the single mom Anna talked about. She works at the bank!

She included a rather annoying thumbs-up emoji.

Kaitlyn is going to get the scoop and I'll keep you posted.

Right. Because no matter what Josh thought he felt, he and Ella weren't friends. She was doing him a favor. Doing his daughter a favor as a way to work through whatever emotions she had left over about her mother's death. Then she was leaving and he would be here. He'd learned too many lessons about what happened when he let someone into his heart. Anna was the only person he truly gave his whole self to because he couldn't help it. She was his heart.

He gave her a return thumbs-up emoji and nearly choked on trying to hide his true feelings, even via text. He should say more. He should tell her to call the whole thing off.

Three dots materialized on the screen, then disappeared, then appeared again, then finally stopped. Disappointment speared through him, and he did his best to tamp it down.

He'd go out with this single mom. With whomever. But he would keep a part of his heart protected because that was the only thing that would keep him safe.

It had been a hard lesson to learn, but he'd finally done it, and he wasn't going to throw it out now.

Chapter Seven

The following Wednesday, Ella parked her car in front of her father's rambling rancher.

She wasn't sure why she'd agreed to come to dinner when she'd been doing a bang-up job of avoiding Jack Samuelson unless it was absolutely necessary.

It probably had something to do with the fact that Josh was out on another date tonight. Sparring with her dad was a better alternative than sulking around her house thinking about Josh with the new single mom in town and whether they would hit it off.

She wanted him to find a woman. The sooner she checked that box off, the sooner she would feel free to move on with her life. Her promise to Anna had quickly come to mean more to Ella than she should let it.

If at the end of this summer Josh hadn't found a woman, at least she would know she'd tried. Her mom would know she'd tried.

She entered the house without knocking because her dad had made it clear this was still her home, even if she didn't want to spend time there.

How could she explain to him all the memories that were encompassed in these walls, both good and bad? She hated admitting the hold the past had over her.

"There's my best girl," Jack said as she walked into the sprawling kitchen with its polished cherry cabinets and granite counters. The scent of roasted garlic and sweet peppers filled the air. The familiarity of it made Ella's stomach lurch.

"You didn't have to cook," she said by way of greeting. "Takeout would have been fine."

The glow in his eyes dimmed for a second, but his smile didn't waver. "Now that I've stepped back from my duties at the bank, I have more time on my hands. I enjoy cooking. I should've helped out your mom more back in the day."

"You should have done a lot of things back in the day," Ella muttered under her breath.

"Can I get you a glass of wine?" Jack asked.

"White, please. A big one."

"Finn will be here any second. Kaitlyn had to go into the city so it will just be the three of us."

Ella took the glass of Pinot Grigio he offered her and downed it in one swallow.

"Rough day?"

"No." She shook her head. "I figure a bit of pre-gaming is a smart idea to prepare for a cozy family dinner."

She wanted him to rise to the bait so she'd have an excuse to act even uglier, but he took every one of her verbal jabs like they were his due.

This version of her father was still disconcerting despite her spending nearly two years back in town. He'd been a cliché of the emotionally distant workaholic parent when she was growing up. It had only gotten worse after her mother's death. Jack had thrown himself into the business of running the bank while leaving Finn and Ella to fend for themselves.

They'd had their physical needs met. He'd been successful enough to hire housekeepers to look after the cleaning and make sure the pantry was stocked. Ella hadn't needed food and clean sheets. She'd craved someone to see how lost she was without her mother. She'd wanted somebody to care for her and had found placeholders in the form of partying friends and a string of bad boyfriends.

Finn had dealt with his own issues, so the siblings hadn't been able to offer each other much solace. And their father had nothing to contribute as far as Ella was concerned.

Finn had found a way of coping, and he'd left Starlight just like she did. But Jack had successfully battled cancer a couple of years ago. His illness was one of the things that originally brought Finn back to their hometown.

Facing his own mortality had changed their hard-nosed father. Ella hadn't believed it when Finn told her, and she had barely been able to accept the fact that her brother had made peace with their dad.

Even returning to Starlight, she knew she never would. It was different for a daughter.

Ella had been a challenge to her gentle mother, but she'd never doubted her mom's love. And she'd been left brokenhearted when Katie died. There was no way she'd open herself to her father after so many years of being disappointed by him.

She couldn't risk it.

Jack refilled her glass as Finn entered the room. "Smells like Mom's homemade spaghetti sauce."

"I thought you both might appreciate it. I have meatballs and pasta, and bread from the bakery."

"I don't eat carbs," Ella announced.

Finn snorted. "I saw you inhale a jelly doughnut the other day."

"Shut up," she said through gritted teeth.

"I wasn't sure about your current eating habits…" Her father grabbed a bowl out of the warming drawer situated under the counter. "So I have spaghetti squash as well, and I made the meatballs in the oven in case you'd prefer a vegetarian meal."

She opened her mouth to make another complaint but couldn't think of one. "Thanks," she said, understanding that she sounded like a begrudging little brat but not caring.

Finn grabbed a beer from the refrigerator along with a big bowl of salad.

Their father brought the food over to the table, and Ella plucked up the bread basket. It was warm and smelled yeasty and delicious. Why in the world had she made a comment about carbs?

"It's okay to take a night off," her father said as she placed the basket on the woven runner. "Both from being carb-free and from hating me. Maybe you could forget both for just an hour or so."

"I don't hate you," she told him. *Hate* was a loaded word and conveyed a level of caring she wasn't willing to admit. "Maybe I'll have one piece of bread."

"That's good," Jack agreed. "Nanci and Mara might ask you if you liked it. Mara suggested the garlic and rosemary flavor when I told her you were coming to dinner."

"Speaking of Mara…" Finn snagged two slices of bread as he slid into the seat across from Ella. "Or at least of Parker. I heard you're trying to find a new girlfriend for his brother."

"Maybe even a wife." Ella tipped up her chin. "Do you think I can't do it?"

The thing about having a popular, capable older brother like Finn was that she'd always felt like she existed in his shadow. Her habit had been to challenge him in everything. Cleaning rooms, grades, sports, anything that could be made a competition she'd found a way to do it. Unfortunately, Ella had almost always lost.

"I think Josh could find a girlfriend on his own. You don't even like him."

"Why do people keep saying that?" Ella took another slice of bread and refused to make eye contact with her father. "We like each other just fine." Toe-curling fine if she was being honest.

"I think it's nice you're helping him," Jack offered as he dished out the food. "Squash or noodles?" he asked Ella.

"Squash," she mumbled as she chewed the bread.

One side of her dad's mouth lifted.

"Your mom would be proud."

The bread turned to sawdust in her mouth.

"She introduced a few of her friends to their husbands," Jack continued. "Had a real knack for knowing when people would fit, and she liked seeing them happy. You obviously take after her."

Ella couldn't even manage a tart response. She was too afraid she'd burst into tears if she tried to speak. Could her typically clueless father even understand how much his words meant to her? Was it possible he was offering her this praise on purpose?

"I visited Mom's statue," she said suddenly.

Both her father and brother stared at her.

"What did you think?" Jack asked after a moment. He'd sat down in his chair and picked up a forkful of meatball but didn't raise it to his mouth.

There were a lot of ways she could answer the

question. That she thought her dad was trying to make up for being a lousy husband when his wife was alive. That she didn't appreciate having to share her mom's memory with anyone who happened upon the memorial. The fact that seeing the statue made the ache of Katie's loss sharp again.

Ella twirled the wineglass between two fingers. "Mom would have liked it," she said quietly.

Her father's shrewd gaze gentled as he nodded.

"Everybody likes it," Finn added, which wasn't the point and both Ella and Jack knew it. "The art festival was a big success, too. I saw the photo that helped Josh's daughter win the award. Kid's got talent."

The conversation turned to the festival grants and news at the bank. Toward the end of the meal, Finn pointed a fork in Ella's direction. "Kaitlyn said you set up Josh with Margerie Winston."

"The new personal banker?" Jack asked.

Ella nodded. "She's also a single mom. It was Anna who suggested her, and Kaitlyn said she's nice."

"She is," Finn said. Somehow those two words held some weighted meaning Ella couldn't quite grasp.

"Great." She held up her hands and ignored the jolt of displeasure that tightened her stomach. "Josh is nice, too. Everyone agrees. Maybe it will be a love match."

"I don't want her to get sucked into some game that—"

"How is my matchmaking for Josh a game? Dad just said Mom used to do the same thing."

"You're not Mom."

Ouch.

"Finn, enough." Jack's voice held a sternness Ella remembered from her teenage years.

"Come on, Dad. I can't be the only one wondering why Hurricane Ella is suddenly turning over this new altruistic leaf." He focused on her again. "Unless you're somehow trying to stir the pot with my friends before you leave town again."

"You really think that?" Her heart pinched right along with her stomach.

"You've been back in Starlight for nearly two years, El. In that time, you haven't made one move to repair relationships with old friends or family, no matter how many olive branches Dad and I have offered you."

"I've been busy."

"With your cooking club? Those women—all of whom are new to town—are the only people you seem to care about. Now that's suddenly changed and you're going to flit about setting up dates for Josh?"

"I don't flit," Ella ground out.

"It just seems out of character."

For her to do something nice for someone. Great. Even her brother thought the worst of her. Her instinct was to push back from the table and flee. Run away from the complex emotions and familiar shame washing through her.

"Stay," her dad said quietly. "Please."

"I'm not going anywhere," she answered just to be contrary once again. She grabbed another slice of bread and settled in for a long, uncomfortable evening.

Two days later, Josh was working at the Dennison Mill patio on initial construction for the pergola that would stretch the entire length of the flagstone space. They wanted to give diners more options for outdoor seating. The food trucks that set up shop around the perimeter had caught on in town and with tourists in the area.

In truth, Mara had only asked him to handle a smaller project on the mill's interior, but he needed a change of scenery from being at the summer camp. A big part of that had to do with Ella, although he wasn't going to admit it.

He'd gone on the date with the single mom she'd picked for him. They'd had a nice dinner and nice conversation and Josh had quickly realized he didn't want nice. He'd been relying on nice for most of his life.

Unassuming had been his survival mechanism when his dad's temper threatened to explode, not that it worked very often. Mac Johnson had little use for anything gentle or nice or unassuming. It was as if he couldn't resist breaking things that seemed fragile, like Josh's mother.

Margerie hadn't exactly been fragile. She was a

single mom, and he admired her story of making a new life for her son, who was a couple of years older than Anna.

They'd connected over shared experiences but agreed at the end of the night that there were no sparks between them and they would be better off parting as potential friends.

He'd picked Anna up from his brother's house after the date and avoided answering detailed questions. No one had seemed particularly surprised that the match hadn't taken.

His daughter hadn't seemed disappointed either, and he thought maybe she'd be satisfied he was at least trying.

He had a feeling Ella wouldn't be satisfied. She'd be piping mad that he hadn't given things with Margerie more of a shot, but he knew they weren't going to work out, so why bother? If he was going to practice with somebody, he'd pick Ella.

He lifted a heavy joist, then turned to find his sister-in-law watching him with a curious expression.

"I'll find somebody eventually," he said before she had a chance to lecture him. He liked Mara. She'd been Josh's friend before she'd fallen for his brother. But he wasn't in the mood to be handled at the moment.

"Sometimes you can waste a lot of hours on people who are right on paper but don't fit in real life. And the person who is the right fit might be the person you least expect."

"I'm not the same as you and Parker."

He hated that an image of Ella's mischievous blue eyes had popped into his mind as Mara spoke. If he'd learned anything from his past, it was the futility of giving his heart to a person who was incapable of loving him back.

His father had been the first and harshest lesson, but his ex-wife had cemented that truth. And hardened his heart in the process.

"Jenn's leaving had more to do with the lack in her than the lack in you," his sister-in-law said as if she could read his mind.

"Is it worth pointing out that you didn't even know my ex-wife? Maybe she had the right idea."

"I didn't know her, but I know you, Josh. I know Anna." She rolled her eyes. "I've met Jenn. Wholly unimpressive."

He chuckled despite himself. "At least she's trying with Anna these days."

"You're always so kind," Mara murmured.

"Not always."

"Anna wants you to be happy."

"I don't like what it says about me that my eight-year-old daughter feels like she needs to worry about my happiness. That's my job."

It was Mara's turn to laugh. "Kids worry about their parents way more than we know. Did being a kid ever stop you from worrying about your mom?"

"That was a different story."

"I know. Just keep an open mind," she urged him.

"You know Ella is leaving at the end of summer. Even if I wanted something to happen with her, it would be pointless."

"Parker was leaving, too, when he and I met."

"What happened to my cynical divorced friend? You and Brynn and I had the perfect single-parent trifecta. Now, I'm the last man standing."

Brynn Dunlap, another Starlight native, had found love with the town's sheriff, her childhood crush, shortly after Parker and Mara got together.

"Maybe that's why Anna is so insistent I find somebody."

"Maybe," Mara agreed. "She's not wrong."

"I'm not sure about that, but I'm giving it my best shot."

It was a lie, but Mara didn't need to know about his half-hearted attempts. Josh couldn't give it his best shot because he wouldn't open his heart that way again. Why should dating be any different?

"We'll see." Mara knew him two well.

"No more talk about Ella and me," he said. "We're not a match. She's the last person on earth I could imagine myself falling for."

He heard the small gasp behind him and cringed.

Mara looked over his shoulder. "Hey, Ella." Mara was terrible at faking brightness. "What brings you to the mill today?"

Josh turned. He wasn't sure what he expected to see in her eyes. Maybe hurt. Maybe vulnerability. Something that would show him he could possibly risk his heart with her. Instead, an icy stare greeted him. Not a surprise, but he hated it all the same.

"You're meeting a new woman at Trophy Room at seven o'clock tonight. I'll be over to watch Anna while you're on the date." Ella said the words like she was being sentenced to a month of hard labor.

It was another reminder of why they could never be anything. She and Anna were too similar.

"I think I need a short break from the fix-ups."

"I didn't ask you to think," she told him. "Just show up at the restaurant. And wear something that makes you look like you're happy to be there."

"Nice to see you, Mara," she said, dismissing him like he was nothing more than a piece of trash stuck to the bottom of her shoe. "I really liked your new lemon chiffon muffins. Perfect for summer."

"Thanks," Mara said, her tone audibly gentler than when she'd been speaking to Josh. Compliments on her baking could always butter up his sister-in-law.

"I'll catch you both later." Ella turned to go.

"Wait." Josh stepped forward and placed a hand on her arm. They both looked down like neither of them could figure out how it had gotten there.

"I think I hear my phone ringing," Mara said into the awkward silence that followed. "I'll make sure the girls save a lemon muffin for you, Ella. Stop by the coffee shop on your way out."

Ella glanced up at Josh as Mara walked away. "I'm on my way out now."

"Don't you want to hear about my date with Margerie?"

"I talked to her. No sparks. I get it. We'll find someone that's a good fit. Somebody who isn't the last person on the planet you'd want to be with."

"You know what I meant by that," he said, even though he couldn't explain the regret making his stomach churn.

One of the workers on the small crew he'd assigned to the mill called out his name.

"Yep," she agreed. "I know what you meant."

Before he could say anything else, she shrugged out of his grasp, turned on her heel and stalked away.

Chapter Eight

Ella ended the call with her former and soon-to-be current supervisor, Bethany Holt, at Traveling Nurses as she pulled into the Tall Pines Camp parking lot Monday morning.

She needed to talk to Kayla Jansen before Bethany called her. Ella had no doubt Bethany would make that call.

Campers wouldn't be arriving for another hour, so the parking lot was empty and the rising sun trailed pink and orange ribbons across the sky. Kayla and Rob lived in the caretaker's cottage during the summer months, and Ella knew the best chance she had at getting Kayla to agree to her plan was catching her before the business of the day consumed her.

She hurried from her car and headed down the path toward the cottage before she lost her nerve. When Kayla answered her knock, Ella held out the box of pastries she'd picked up from the coffee shop. "Hi," she said softly. "I need to talk to you."

"Who's there?" she heard Rob call from inside the cabin.

"Ella brought us breakfast from Main Street Perk," Kayla answered, glancing at the box but not taking it from Ella.

"Hot damn," Rob shouted. "That a girl."

Kayla smiled. "Come on in and say a proper good-morning. I need coffee and then we'll talk."

Ella followed her to the kitchen. Kayla had been friends with Ella's mom back in the day and had treated Ella with so much kindness, even when she was going through her rough, rebellious patch during high school.

"Hey, kid." Rob waved from his spot at the table reading the morning newspaper. "Heard you helped out with the little Johnson girl the other day. Thanks for that."

"My pleasure." Ella must have put too much oomph into the words because both Kayla and Rob startled, then exchanged a look she couldn't interpret.

"I'm guessing by your enthusiasm that you've already started on the caffeine this morning." Kayla pulled two mugs out of the cabinet.

"I did," Ella said. "I didn't sleep well last night and needed a pick-me-up." She didn't mention that her lack of sleep was because every time she closed her eyes and drifted off, she had the most annoying recurring sex dream featuring Josh.

She'd actually considered setting up an online dating profile for herself so she could swipe right and take the edge off. Okay, that was a lie. She didn't want a random hookup. Unfortunately, she wanted Josh.

Task at hand, she commanded herself. "I wanted to talk to you about a job," she said as Kayla handed her the mug. She took the tiniest sip of the dark, rich brew. She'd guzzled a large coffee from Main Street Perk on the way up the mountain and her whole body tingled with caffeine jitters.

"Honey, we're giving you as much work as we have."

"You're doing a great job of it, too," Rob added, folding his paper and placing it on the table. "Those house network stars would be impressed with your ability to paint. Such clean lines."

"Thank you." Ella smiled at the gentle giant of a man. Rob had been the kind of dad she'd yearned for growing up—all bear hugs and shirts with funny slogans that made kids laugh. Nothing like her business-first father. "I wanted to talk to you about a nursing job."

Just saying the words made her stomach roll like a boat in a stormy sea. "You'd said something about Susan needing to take extra time to take care of her father?"

Kayla frowned. "She mentioned reducing her hours so she could commute between here and Spokane while he's in rehab after his hip surgery. But we already offered you that job, and you declined."

"Offered it to you for two summers straight," Rob added.

"I know. And I don't have a right to request this now. But you know I'm starting up with Traveling Nurses again at the end of the summer. I guess there are a few people within the organization who are worried about me coming back since I've taken a break from working in health care. My supervisor thought it would be a good idea if I add some recent experience this summer." She glanced down at the coffee, but even caffeine couldn't make this conversation easier. "I might have told her I was working for you guys."

"You told her you're already working for us?" Kayla clarified. "As a nurse?"

Just then, the phone sitting in the center of the counter began to both vibrate and ring.

"Don't answer," Ella pleaded. Embarrassment washed through her. She didn't want anyone to know how anxious she felt about going back to nursing and her doubts about her ability to function at the level she used to in high-pressure situations.

She thought she'd made it clear to her bosses that she'd needed time away to recharge and spend time with her father after his illness, which was pushing the limits of the truth to its furthest edge. Her continued delays in returning had obviously tipped them off that something more was going on and the fact she was not anywhere near fine, let alone refreshed and relaxed in the way she'd reported.

"Please, Kayla. You know I'm a good nurse. I can help."

The other woman made a show of opening the box from the coffee shop until the phone went silent. "Rob, she got you an apple fritter."

"My favorite."

Kayla flashed a smile at Ella, then turned to her husband. "Why don't you take it to go so you can make sure the counselors are getting all the equipment ready for the climbing wall. No accidents today."

Ella felt her cheeks burn as the big man pushed away from the table.

"I think that's a great idea, honey."

He plucked up the fritter and took the paper towel Kayla handed him and then gave Ella a one-armed hug. "You two ladies will get this worked out. Of that I have no doubt."

Ella had no doubt she was in for one of Kayla's well-meaning but unnecessary lectures on life.

Kayla took a dainty bite from one of the scones. "You know I've been baking for over thirty years and I still can't get anywhere near to what Mara can do with a few simple ingredients. That woman has a gift. You want one?"

"No thanks." Ella had a feeling one bite would send her stomach into even more turmoil.

"You have a gift, too, my dear. A gift for taking care of people. For nursing. But I also know you're still dealing with a lot from losing your mom the way you did. It was hardest on you."

Ella shook her head. "How can you say that? Finn was with her when she died. Nothing could compare to that."

"You were her daughter. I'm not diminishing the trauma your brother experienced, but it's different for a daughter to lose her mother in such a tragic way on the cusp of becoming a woman. Your mother was so proud of you and had amazing dreams for your life."

"Then you're probably happy to hear I'm getting back to nursing," Ella suggested with as much cheer as she could muster. "That would have made Mom proud. More than me cleaning cabins and taking random jobs in town like I have no career path."

"Those globe-trotting nurses are lucky to have you. Your patients are, too. But my concern is for you, baby girl. I don't know the details of why you came back to town or how we've gotten so lucky to have you stay for so long. You know this is your home no matter how many countries you travel to. Starlight is the place where you belong."

Ella didn't bother to argue. Kayla already saw too much with her gentle eyes and easy smile. Ella wasn't willing to reveal any more.

"It's okay if you don't want me working with the

counselors and guests here," she said, ignoring the flash of pain when Kayla didn't immediately deny it.

Ella picked up her coffee cup and took a big swig, then carried it to the sink. "There's a nursing shortage in town." She repeated Tessa's words. "I'm sure I could find per diem work at the hospital."

"We want you here."

Kayla came up behind Ella and rested her chin on Ella's shoulder. She was enveloped in the scent of white musk perfume, Kayla's signature scent.

"I'll talk to whoever you want me to. Just know you don't have to keep running around this big earth to do good in the world. You don't have to do anything to earn the love your mother would have freely given to you. You and Finn were her heart, and your daddy was her soul."

Ella sniffed. "How sad for her."

"Jack loved Katie," Kayla said in a tone that Ella didn't dare question. "He made some mistakes. What man doesn't? What person doesn't? But he and your mom were happy in their own way. I know that didn't do a lot for you once she was gone, but he's doing better."

"Good for him," Ella said flippantly. "It doesn't matter to me. I'm leaving."

"I think it does matter. I think it's part of the reason you came back in the first place. Relationships are precious and there are no guarantees in life. Your mom was taken from us in an instant and far too soon. That loss didn't serve to change your father in the way I would've hoped at the time, but cancer did the job."

She drew back, turning Ella so they faced each other. "Give him a chance."

"Dad and I are fine. I went over there for dinner the other night with Finn. Nobody even slammed out the door."

The phone rang again. Kayla glanced at it, then back at Ella. "You go on and get settled in the nurse's office. I'll have Susan call you and the two of you can work out how you want to divide hours and duties. I'm going to tell whoever this is on the phone what I told you. That they are lucky to have Ella Samuelson, but she belongs to the people who love her."

"Thank you," Ella whispered as tears burned her throat. After giving Kayla a quick hug, she rushed out of the cabin before she completely lost it.

Josh recognized the lone figure sitting at the end of the dock as he walked toward the cabin where he was working an hour later.

Keep walking, he told himself, even though he felt as though he needed to make amends for his last-person-on-earth comment. She probably didn't care one bit. Ella had made it clear she wanted nothing to do with him beyond sourcing a girlfriend.

He liked to think that along with the pain that had come from being rejected by both his father and his former wife, there had been some positives, too.

Namely he'd learned to protect his heart.

Walk away.

It would be the smart thing to do. He had no doubt it's what Ella would have done if she'd seen him alone, shoulders slumped forward and head in his hands like it was too much to keep it upright.

Keep on moving.

Instead, he walked toward her. Tiny waves lapped at the shore, and rows of sunny yellow kayaks and forest green canoes waited for campers to climb in and paddle across the lake.

Josh wished there had been someplace like Tall Pines when he was a kid—a refuge from his father's anger and abuse. He'd never known during the summer when his dad would show up in the middle of the afternoon, his cruelty on full display.

Mac had sold insurance in addition to his duties as town mayor. Sometimes when he was having a rough day, he liked to come home for a nap and a beer and to terrorize his wife and kids.

The start of each school year was Josh's favorite time because those were the only hours when he felt truly safe. The dock creaked as he approached, but Ella's posture didn't change.

He sat down next to her and unfolded his legs over the edge. His feet dangled inches above the lake's surface. For a few minutes, they sat in a comfortable silence looking out over the clear water.

"Anna said you make better mac and cheese than

me," he told her eventually. "I want you to know that's high praise coming from my daughter."

Ella offered a whisper of a smile. "That's funny because the whole time I was making it, she sat at the counter and critiqued my effort. She's going to be a handful when she's a teenager."

"Don't I know it."

"Is that part of your girlfriend criteria—somebody who will be able to manage Anna?"

He rolled his shoulders. "Hell, no."

Ella scoffed. "You mean to tell me you aren't considering the relationship your potential love interest will have with your daughter? Come on. The whole reason you're doing this is for Anna, or part of the reason at least. Maybe you're also doing it because you're finally ready to end the dry spell after your dumb wife left you."

"My dumb ex-wife," he corrected. "And, of course, I'm thinking about Anna. It's important to me that any woman I date get along with her. But I'm not looking for someone to manage her. I want a person who can encourage her and be a role model for her and celebrate her feisty spirit. Nobody is going to manage my kid."

Ella nudged him with her arm. "You never cease to impress. You should write that little speech down and give it to any woman you meet. Who wouldn't want a guy who respects his daughter at that level?"

"As a matter of fact, my most recent date had

some very interesting thoughts about the difference in raising girls and boys."

"Tell me you mean that in a good way."

"I mean she's a big believer that boys should be boys and girls should be seen and not heard."

"How is that possible? She's a single mom."

"Of a boy who lost what she deemed an unfair class election to his female counterpart at his last school."

"You are joking." Ella's eyes narrowed. "Did that woman say one negative word about Anna?"

"Not exactly. She might have mentioned something about the importance of teaching kids self-control so they don't have accidents."

"I will take her out," Ella told him.

The offer was said with such vehemence, it made him smile. "Pump the brakes, wild woman. I let her know that I would parent my child as I see fit and keep encouraging Anna to be brave."

"I'm still going to have words with her. Trust me, my mom got all kinds of well-meaning advice when I was a kid about how to rein me in. After she was gone, all those women stopped being helpful and outright gossiped about me. I'm not saying that Anna is going to follow in my footsteps. I was way out of control. But don't let anyone make you feel like your kid isn't perfect."

"Nobody's perfect, and I don't expect that of Anna. I want to give her the space to fail and learn from her mistakes."

"Seriously, if you aren't using your philosophy on raising a daughter as a pickup line, you're missing out on a golden opportunity. It's sexy as heck."

He leaned closer. "Women's empowerment," he said in a low voice. "Beyoncé forever. Ruth Bader Ginsburg is my idol."

Ella burst out laughing. "Now you're laying it on too thick."

"Come on. RBG was hot. All the cool cats think so."

"You should never say the phrase 'cool cats' again."

"This is why I need your guidance." Josh glanced over his shoulder to make sure they were still alone, then cupped a hand on Ella's cheek and kissed her. "And more practice," he said against her soft lips.

She opened for him, deepening their connection. Immediately his body revved up while his heart seemed to settle peacefully.

Ella's small sigh of pleasure ignited a fire inside him. He wanted more, to hear every sound she'd make if he explored her body.

"I don't have any other candidates lined up at the moment," Ella said when she broke away from him.

He breathed out a laugh. "I'm not exactly thinking about other women at the moment."

A blush colored her cheeks. "You're really good at the charm thing in your own way. I've taught you well."

"I'm not trying to charm you, Ella." He ran a hand

through his hair and looked across the lake. "I like hanging out with you. It's easy."

"No strings," she agreed, and he heard a note of tension in her voice that clued him in not to argue with her.

He could be himself around Ella, but it wasn't about strings. She was fun and funny, and he liked her more than he was willing to admit to either of them.

"Do you want to come over for dinner Saturday night?" he asked.

One delicate brow rose. "Why?"

"To brainstorm possible dates," he said, the lie sitting heavy in his stomach. "You can give me feedback on my online profiles."

She gasped. "You have dating profiles?"

Now his face heated with embarrassment. "I've never really used them, but Parker made me set up a couple when he came back to town. He was convinced I needed to get…" Josh cleared his throat. "To get out into the dating world again."

"Right." Ella grinned. "Yes, I'll come to dinner and we'll get you updated. I bet your profile picture is awful."

The last thing Josh wanted to do was to spend the evening looking at dating apps with Ella. But what he did want was worse—to spend the evening just enjoying her company.

This was why he didn't bother dating. His self-preservation instincts were absolute trash. There were plenty of available women in the world, and he wasn't going to fall for one who didn't like kids—his in particular—and wasn't sticking around long-term.

"Great." He stood up and offered her a hand. "I'm sure the perfect match for me is just waiting for a swipe."

Chapter Nine

"Have you considered that these setups aren't working because you're picking the wrong women on purpose?"

Without thinking, Ella threw the warm roll she'd just picked up at Madison's head, wishing it was stale and hard.

Madison's hand came up, and she batted away the yeasty projectile. "Rude, and you can't have another."

Ella plucked another roll from the tray and licked it. She was back on carbs with a vengeance.

"Your childish behavior only proves I'm right."

"You're not," Ella insisted and bit off a piece of chewy deliciousness. The lunch crowd at Trophy

Room was in for quite a treat with Madison's special meat loaf and home-baked rolls.

Ella had decided to stay in town the day of her scheduled dinner with Josh as a way to distract herself from him. The way he kissed her. The way his smile did funny things to her insides. The fact that she was determined to find the perfect woman for him when what she wanted was to be that woman herself. "I don't want Josh," she said as much to herself as to Madison.

She wasn't convincing either of them.

She'd come to the bar to visit her friend, figuring Madison could talk some sense into her, but her heart and body weren't in the mood to be discouraged.

"Not long-term, anyway," she clarified. "I mean, he's cute enough."

"Lumberjack hot." Madison made a show of fanning herself. "All that flannel and a bit of scruff. I bet he's a great hugger."

"Do you even like hugs?"

Madison laughed as she stirred the tomato sauce simmering on the stove of Trophy Room's kitchen. "No, but if I did, I'd want a strong hug, you know?"

"Yeah," Ella murmured. She didn't consider herself much of a cuddler either, but she had an annoyingly recurrent fantasy about snuggling into Josh and burying her face in the crook of his neck. She just bet he'd smell amazing, like the woods and the best kind of spices and security. "For the record, you were supposed to be my safe space. If I'd wanted someone to talk romance with me, I would have called Cory or Tessa. You don't believe in love."

Madison wrinkled her nose and tucked a stray lock of pale blond hair behind one ear. "True, but I believe in good sex, and I think Josh would be darn good in bed."

"You have no reason to think that."

"He's kind and thoughtful and great with his hands. Those skills are transferable."

"I don't want to have sex with Josh."

She turned at the sound of a choked laugh to find Jordan Shaeffer, Trophy Room's handsome owner, standing behind her in the doorway that led to the bar's office. "I'm going to pretend I didn't hear that."

"We need a male point of view," Madison said, gesturing him forward.

"No, we don't." Ella shook her head. "You were supposed to take my mind off of Josh. I don't want to think about him sweaty and naked between the sheets."

Jordan groaned. "You and me both, Ella. I'm just going to walk through the kitchen without another word."

"How would you describe a woman who would be Josh's perfect date?" Madison demanded.

"See me walking quietly and quickly?" Jordan grimaced. "I'm practically running."

"I'll follow you," Madison told him. "You can't escape."

"That's what I'm afraid of."

Ella waited as Jordan took a few deep breaths. He concentrated on the floor in front of him like the answers to all of life's deepest secrets were contained in the scuffs of the old oak.

"Josh is a good guy," he said after what seemed like an eternity. "He deserves a good woman."

"Deep thoughts with the barman," Madison said, laughing. "Ella has the basics covered. Good man. Good woman. Yadda, yadda. You're his friend, right?"

Jordan nodded, glancing between the two women like a prisoner might face a firing squad. "His ex-wife messed with him pretty badly. I don't think I'm giving away any state secrets by telling you that."

"She was the definition of 'didn't deserve him,'" Ella confirmed.

"So someone who isn't like Jenn, who could love his daughter and this town and isn't into drama. No drama."

Madison growled in her throat. "Your insight is riveting, boss, and also as boring as watching paint dry. When I think of a woman at Josh's side, I see someone sweet and adorable. She bakes homemade cookies and puts out way too many holiday decorations. I would not be friends with her."

Ella refused to meet Madison's gaze even when she could feel it on her.

"Well, you'd be wrong," Jordan said without hesitation.

Ella felt her eyes widen. That's exactly how she

would have described Josh's perfect woman as well, so it shocked her that one of his friends disagreed.

"Enlighten us," Madison prompted as she continued prepping several of the menu items. The afternoon hour was a short respite from the everyday bustle of the kitchen with only the chef working.

"Josh can make his own cookies, and he's kind of a minimalist when it comes to decorating. A lot of people in this town think they have him pegged. The boy next door and everyone's best friend or whatever. But there's more to him, an edge that a lot of us don't see. It's there, and if I were going to choose his ideal woman, I'd pick someone who made him comfortable enough to own that part of himself."

Jordan massaged a hand over the back of his neck. "It's also no secret that his dad was a real piece of work. Josh tamped down his personality to try to keep the peace. He needs someone who makes him feel safe enough to take some risks. A woman who pushes him a little. He'd be bored to tears with the Susie Homemaker type. Those are the kind of women everyone wants to see him with."

"But not you," Ella said slowly.

"I want to see him happy, and I don't think that's going to do it."

The three of them stood in silence as Ella and Madison absorbed Jordan's insight.

"We appreciate your opinion," the chef said finally. "Right, Ella?"

"Yes," she said, trying to come up with more

words to string together around the pounding in her head. "I'll make sure to rule out anyone who is too domestic."

Jordan barked out a laugh. "Domestic is okay. Just not vanilla."

"I pegged Josh for a vanilla guy," Madison admitted.

"Most people do," Jordan agreed. "But he's Rocky Road all the way."

Ella's heart crashed against her rib cage with so much force she was surprised Jordan and Madison couldn't hear it pounding. *Calm down*, she commanded herself. But she couldn't ignore the fact that Rocky Road happened to be her very favorite.

She showed up at Josh's house that night in her rattiest jeans and a plain white tank top. Her hair was pulled back in a still-wet bun from the shower she'd taken earlier, and she'd purposely not worn a stitch of makeup.

It wasn't as if this was a date, she'd reminded herself when her fingers had itched to swipe on at least a bit of mascara. She'd never been the type to dress to impress, but this was taking it to a different level. Heck, she'd taken more care with her appearance when she was painting the cabins at the camp.

She rang the doorbell and glanced around at the clean front porch with two white rocking chairs in front of the picture window.

When Josh opened the door, his eyes widened as

he took her in. "Wow, you look amazing," he said without a trace of irony.

"You're joking," she told him, almost wanting to take a step back.

"Not at all." His grin was genuine as his eyes darkened with an emotion she refused to name. "You're stunning, Ella. You have to know that. A woman who can look as gorgeous as you do without even trying is a true beauty."

Her mouth dropped open even as desire skittered along her spine. "You can't stay stuff like that to me. Enough with the charm," she commanded, then shoved the bag she held toward him when he would have argued with her. She didn't have the strength to keep her defenses shored against his inherent kindness.

Ella had never been a big fan of kindness in the men she chose. She gravitated toward the bad boys and rebels, and while she knew that didn't necessarily mean that they were men who treated women poorly, those were the ones she wanted.

Until now.

"It's vanilla," she said when Josh peeked into the bag. "I like vanilla ice cream. It's my favorite. Classic without overdoing it. No other flavor is as good."

"Um…okay," he said slowly.

"Vanilla is my favorite, too," Anna said as she appeared at Josh's side. "Dad likes Rocky Road. He thinks vanilla is boring. He always tries to add chocolate syrup or crushed-up graham crackers."

"Another thing we don't have in common," Ella said triumphantly. Triumphant in the lie, anyway.

"Are we talking about ice cream or something else?" Josh asked as he took a step back to let her in.

"Do you like chocolate or vanilla cake?" Anna asked Ella as they walked through the house. Ella couldn't help but notice that it was, indeed, fairly sparse when it came to knickknacks or clutter. Interesting, because she would have somehow expected Josh to live in comfortable chaos instead of a minimalist haven.

Anna looked at her expectantly. "You can't choose both."

"Vanilla," Ella said. Her actual favorite was red velvet.

"Dad likes chocolate."

He shrugged as he headed toward the freezer with the carton of ice cream. "I like pie the best."

"We aren't even talking about pie," Ella shouted, then swallowed hard when both Josh and Anna stared at her like she'd just sprouted a unicorn horn out of her forehead.

"Rough day?" Josh asked.

"It was fine," she said, her tone purposefully even. "Sorry, for a moment I felt like I was in a *Gilmore Girls* episode with all of the random banter. I was never a fan of that show."

"I don't know anyone named Gilmore," Anna said, her adorable curls bouncing. "But I don't like fruit pie if that makes you feel better about freaking out."

Ella nodded. "It does. Thank you." She saw Josh try to hide his smile, and her heart started that pounding again. This one conversation had probably ruined her for dessert for the rest of her life.

"I'm going to start the grill." Josh pointed at the refrigerator. "Help yourself to a drink. Hopefully, lemonade and juice boxes aren't a trigger for you."

Ella made sure Anna was looking in the other direction, then flipped him a one-figured salute.

He laughed, deep and low.

Damn her body for reacting to every little thing this man did.

"Daddy, can you drop me off at Aubrey's house before you start cooking?" Anna asked, looking up from her coloring at the kitchen table. "I'm almost done with her birthday card."

"Birthday card?"

Ella almost giggled at the look of confusion on Josh's handsome face.

"It's her sleepover party." Anna beamed at him. "Remember, my first sleepaway other than Evie. Her mommy is doing spa night and we're going to have face masks and paint our toes and a sundae bar. It will be the coolest thing ever."

"That's tonight?" Josh glanced toward Ella. "But we have a dinner guest."

"She's not here for me." Anna shook her head.

"I'm here to help pick out a perfect woman for

your dad to date," Ella said quickly. She didn't want to give the girl the wrong impression, like Ella had the hots for Anna's father.

"I know." Anna hopped up from the table. "You're not doing too good so far, and Michael said his mommy thought Daddy was too indulge tent. I told her we haven't been camping once this summer."

"Indulgent," Josh muttered.

"Going to have words with her," Ella said under her breath.

"We'll go camping next weekend, Banana. But I'm not sure about this birthday party sleepover. What if I pick you up after all of the spa fun?"

"You promised I could go."

"Is Evie going?"

Anna looked at the floor. "She wasn't invited."

"Okay," Josh agreed, reluctance clear in his tone. "Do you have a gift for her?"

Anna nodded enthusiastically. "I got a set of Legos out of the gift closet."

Ella lifted a brow. "You have a gift closet?"

The girl picked up her card and put the lid on the small bin that held the crayons. "Daddy sometimes forgets birthdays and stuff so now we have a box in the closet with all kinds of gifts in it."

Josh looked mildly embarrassed at this admission, which Ella found adorable at the same time she was irritated by her reaction. "I can drop Anna at the party," she offered.

"But you can't get out of the car," Anna said.

"Daddy always gets out of the car to talk, and I'm too old for that now."

"Eight going on eighteen," Josh agreed. He stepped toward his daughter and wrapped her in a tight hug.

Madison would have appreciated that hug, Ella mused. She didn't want to admit how much she did as well.

"I think I agreed to this party in a moment of weakness," he said, smoothing a hand over his daughter's silky hair. "Just remember that I'm only a phone call away. If anything happens, you have my number memorized."

"I'll get my bag and the gift," Anna said excitedly. "This is gonna be so much fun."

She disappeared from the kitchen, and her foot-falls pounded up the stairs.

"It's a birthday sleepover," she said. "She isn't flying off to Vegas for a bachelorette party."

"But she will someday." Josh groaned. "This is the first step. It's hard to watch my baby grow up."

Ella thought about her father for a moment. In her mind, she figured Jack had been relieved when she'd gone off to college. Relieved that she'd not done ir-revocable damage to her future with her stupid teen-age choices.

Had it been bittersweet for him? Was Kayla right about his emotions being deeper than Ella gave him credit for?

"You're a good dad," she said.

"But I'm great at grilling steaks," he told her with a wink. "Bring your appetite back with you."

He gave her the address of the girl who was having the party, and it only took about ten minutes to reach the house.

"Remember you can't get out," Anna said as Ella pulled to a stop in front of the curb.

"No chance of that." Ella took in the small posse of moms standing in the front yard while a half dozen girls sprinted around them. "Although I'm sure these women don't mind your daddy getting out to talk to them."

Anna put her hand on the back of the seat.

"Mara says they're thirsty, although a lot of the mommies are always drinking coffee or their mom juice so I don't know why they'd be thirsty."

Ella smiled at the slang term, which meant those women were desperate for something. Probably Josh.

"What in the world is mom juice?"

"I think it's wine."

"Then they should call it wine."

"That's what Daddy says, too. *Mom juice* sounds fancier."

"It sounds ridiculous."

Ella turned to face the girl. "Remember what your dad said. I'm sure tonight will be fun, but if you're at all uncomfortable, you call him."

Anna rolled her eyes. "I know. Do you have some other women in mind for him to date because I think it makes him sad when things don't work out when he goes out with somebody? I don't like it when he's sad."

Another direct hit to Ella's heart. What the heck had happened to all of her defense mechanisms? Josh and Anna seemed to be able to crash through them with no effort at all.

"We'll find somebody perfect," she promised the girl. Anna nodded then let herself out of the car. Ella didn't bother waving to the mom brigade. She had no reason to try to get to know any of those women. She was leaving and she wasn't one of them.

Although her heart ached in an odd way as she returned to Josh's house. She realized she'd looked forward to spending the evening with Anna and trading barbs with her as much as she was glad to have more time with Josh.

The thought only strengthened her resolve to find somebody for him. She'd returned to Starlight and managed to spend nearly two years without allowing anybody but the women from her cooking club to get close.

Now her time here was winding down. Between Josh and her dad, she was starting to question why she wanted to leave in the first place. Which meant she had to get out before her doubts became more than she could handle.

Chapter Ten

Ella Samuelson ate like an NFL linebacker, and Josh loved every second of it. Not that he was fool enough to point it out to her, and the football reference might be an exaggeration.

But during the couple of dates he'd been on recently, it had almost pained him how the women across the table picked at their food like tiny birds, as if there was some adult-dating manual that advised eating was unattractive.

He couldn't think of anything more appealing than the way Ella's face had softened when she'd taken the first bite of the steak he'd grilled. She'd closed her eyes and moaned in approval, swaying slightly like his effort was worthy of a Michelin star.

Josh had gone speechless, although his body had been silently shouting at him to step up to the plate.

"Are you kidding me with this?" Ella pointed her fork between him and the piece of strawberry freezer pie she was halfway through eating. "I don't like pie and this is amazing. Did Mara teach you everything she knows or what?"

He shrugged, although he couldn't hide his proud smile at her compliment. "Anna and I watch *The Great British Baking Show*. I've picked up a couple of pointers over the last several seasons."

He resisted the urge to squirm when she stared at him, her full lips parted slightly.

"Does that make me sound like too much of a wimp? Because I know all about toxic masculinity, and I'm not interested in it. That was my dad's deal. I'm not looking for a woman who can't handle a man knowing the difference between baking soda and baking powder."

Ella still didn't answer but pushed away from the table and rose from her chair. For a moment, he thought she was going to walk out. Then she came around to him, placed her hands on either side of his face and leaned down to kiss him.

"Say the words *baking powder* again," she commanded with a teasing lift to one corner of her mouth. "It's a real turn-on."

He adjusted his chair to face her, opened his legs and drew her between his knees. "Baking powder," he said, grinning. "Active dry yeast. All-purpose flour."

She moaned softly and climbed into his lap. Josh would have continued with the strange sexy-times talk but couldn't formulate a thought with Ella pressed against him.

She was soft in the places he wasn't and all his brain could think was that he wanted more.

Their tongues mingled, and he moved his hands up and down her back, cursing the thin layer of fabric that separated the two of them.

He wanted more. He needed more. He needed—

"It's practice," she said as if reading his thoughts. "You should be ready for what comes next."

"Yes, I should," he agreed, even though he could not have cared less about what came next or another date or his future or anything outside of this moment and this woman.

He lifted her and turned toward the table, pushing aside the remaining dishes, which clattered to the floor.

Ella's eyes widened as he laid her back on the wood. "I've only seen that move in movies."

"It's a first for me, too," he admitted because he could say that to her without worrying what she would think about him.

It was as if the more he let her see who he truly was and the more she revealed herself to him, the closer he felt to her.

He could do it because it didn't have to mean anything. She was leaving. That's what he told himself. That's what he would tell anyone stupid enough to ask. Whether or not it was the truth didn't matter. Not at the moment.

He'd only been with a couple of women before he'd met his ex-wife. In all of his previous relationships, he'd kept things slow and under control— whether on purpose or because he was as boring as Jenn had accused him of being, he didn't know. But there was no going slow right now.

Ella seemed to feel the same way because she grabbed the hem of her tank top and whipped it over her head, then reached for his T-shirt and tugged it up. "Tell me you have protection."

He nodded. "Ella, are we—"

"No talking. You need practice, and I need to get this out of my system."

He should be offended by that. He was something she wanted to be rid of, but he couldn't bring himself to care. Not when she reached behind her back, her perfect breasts jutting toward him, and then unfastened the clasp of her bra.

She gave a shaky laugh. "If you look at a woman like that—as if she's the most amazing thing you've ever seen…well, that's going to work to your advantage."

"You are the most amazing thing I've ever seen."

She shook her head. "Save the charm. Here's a hint—I'm a sure thing right now."

He didn't contradict her. Somehow he knew if he

revealed too much, it would ruin what was between them. In addition to this thundering desire, he also enjoyed hanging out with her. She was feisty and argumentative and was quickly becoming one of his best friends.

Which showed him to be a complete idiot because their lives didn't mesh on a variety of levels. Not the least of which was that she didn't want to be a part of Anna's life, although his daughter had seemed more than willing to have Ella take her to the party tonight. It was as if Ella and his daughter had some sort of mutual understanding, drawn to each other like magnets even though one turn and they would gladly push each other away.

Or maybe he was a fool because he was overanalyzing life when he should be living in the moment.

He had a gorgeous woman half-naked in front of him and—

"You don't have a dad bod," she told him, biting down on her bottom lip in a way that had all the blood in his head rushing south.

"This is a dad bod," he countered, flicking open the top button on his shorts. "It's the body I have."

"But right now, it's mine." She crooked a finger and he moved closer again. Ella scooted to the edge of the table as she ran her hands up his chest. He leaned in and nipped at her earlobe, then kissed the soft skin of her neck.

She turned her head and brushed her tongue along the seam of his lips, then it felt like Ella was the one doing the claiming as their kiss went molten hot again. Josh was happy to let her lead the way until it felt as though his control was slipping.

He would make this good for her—for both of them—but he was a sure thing at this point. He broke the kiss and moved his attention to first one puckered nipple and then the other. Her skin was soft and tasted like vanilla, and Josh couldn't imagine anything more delicious.

She arched into him, and he hissed out a breath as her nails dug into his shoulders.

"More," she commanded in a husky tone and allowed him to help her out of her jeans and panties.

He took a step back just to admire her beauty. Had he ever seen anything so… "Perfect."

Twin spots of color bloomed on her cheeks. "Not from where I'm sitting," she told him, sounding every inch the commanding goddess he knew her to be. "Lose the shorts."

Happy to oblige, Josh first grabbed his wallet from the counter and took out a condom. Parker had given him a box as a gift after his divorce. Subtlety had never been one of his brother's strengths. It had taken about six months before Josh even placed one in his wallet, and he'd never had cause to use it until now.

He owed his brother a beer.

He slipped on the condom as he returned to Ella, then reached out to trail one finger from her breasts down her stomach to the apex of her thighs.

"Perfect," he repeated as he dipped inside her and had the satisfaction of watching her eyes go hazy with pleasure. His fingers moved in and over her swollen flesh until she was gasping with need.

It felt like his whole body reacted to each sound she made, every pulse of her hips. He'd never wanted anything or anyone more than he did Ella at this moment. She groaned and clutched the edge of the table, then reached for him.

"Not by myself," she said on a hoarse breath. "Inside me, Josh. Now."

He didn't have to be told twice and moved his hand back to her breast as he entered her in one smooth stroke.

Ella considered herself a modern woman. Although she'd given up promiscuity after her rebellious high school phase, she had a healthy view of sex.

It was nice. Great on occasion.

But being with Josh was something different. Something more. And utterly terrifying.

As they moved together, she tried to remember this was physical and nothing more.

His body fit with hers like they were made to be together, but that didn't account for the sensation in her heart as he dropped tender kisses on her neck. Josh managed the perfect combination of desperate need and slow seduction. He claimed her like he couldn't get enough but still made her feel like she was precious to him. It embarrassed her how much she liked the feeling.

She was independent and prided herself on not needing anyone. Needing led to pain, and she'd had enough of that to last a lifetime.

Josh made her believe she was safe in his arms and that gave her a heady freedom she loved. It was like nothing she'd ever felt.

But there was no time to overanalyze as the pressure built deep inside her. Her entire body tingled, and it felt as though she was racing toward a finish line with nothing but pleasure propelling her forward. Then the dam broke and light spilled over her in a million brilliant sparks.

It lit her up from the inside out in a way she'd never experienced before. She hadn't even gathered herself together when Josh shattered and ground out his own release. She held him tight as he kissed her, their breath mingling until she wasn't sure where she ended and he began. She'd never felt so close to another person in her life.

It would scare her when the moment was over. She knew enough about herself to realize that, but right now she reveled in it. She loved the feeling of being connected with him, and not just their bodies. Because it felt as though their bond reached all the way to her soul.

"I feel like I owe you an apology," he said after a few moments.

"What for?" She pushed at his chest. "The best orgasm of my life?"

He lifted himself from her and held up one finger. "Hold that thought." Then he hurried off to the bathroom that sat next to the kitchen.

Ella took a few moments to compose herself, which included snapping her bra into place and putting on her discarded underpants and jeans. As she dressed, she glanced around the homey—if uncluttered—space. There were colored drawings and school photos on the refrigerator, a pink backpack sitting on the counter, and she'd just had sex on the table.

On a table. Never had she ever even dreamed of doing anything so spontaneous.

She bent to begin cleaning up the broken dishes when Josh reappeared. "Don't do that. I'll take care of it. I made the mess."

"We made the mess," she corrected. "At least I really liked you making the mess. I'm not going to apologize for it. You shouldn't either."

"I should have taken you into the bedroom." A blush stained his cheeks. "That's what I want to apologize to you for."

She straightened and stepped toward him until they were standing toe-to-toe. "Listen, Johnson. None of this regrets stuff—for the table or any of it. You can invite me to dinner and make a mess of your kitchen and thoroughly pleasure me anytime you want."

"Thoroughly?" A teasing light shone in his eyes.

"From my head to my feet. This was the best time I've had in forever."

He lifted his hand and ran his thumb over her lips. "Did it get me out of your system as intended?"

It left Ella wanting more if truth be told. But she wasn't about to share that truth.

"Totally," she answered.

His smile widened. "You're a terrible liar."

Before she could double down on the lie, his phone rang from the counter.

"That could be Anna," he said as the sound filled the air.

He plucked up the device. "Hello? Hey, Banana. What's going on? Yes, absolutely. You can tell me about it when I get there."

Ella took a step closer to him, unease tingling along her spine. "Is she okay?"

"I think so, but she wants me to come and get her at the party."

"She's only been there…" Ella glanced at the clock on the wall. "Barely two hours."

"I know, but now she's done. I'll find out more when she's with me." She could hear the tension in his voice despite the fact that outwardly he looked calm. He'd started pulling on his clothes as he answered the call and now shoved his feet into the sneakers discarded under the table.

He glanced at the remnants of dinner still scattered across the floor.

"It's fine." Ella made a shooing motion with her hands. "Go get Anna. I'll take care of cleaning up."

"I'm—"

She held up a finger. "No apologies. We're friends, right? This is what friends do."

He looked like he wanted to argue. She would have appreciated that because what she felt for Josh was quickly becoming far more serious than friendship.

"Friends," he repeated. "Just don't leave. We're not done here."

The message was like an icy bucket of water dumped over her head. They weren't done because they hadn't gone over the dating apps. She was still committed to helping him find someone else. Even though the thought of it appealed to her as much as sticking a fork in her eye.

"I'll be here," she said, but he was already halfway out the door.

Chapter Eleven

An hour later, Josh paced from one end of his living room to the other. He stopped and glanced up at the ceiling where Anna's room was situated above them on the second floor. "There is nothing worse than having a sad kid."

"It's rough," Ella agreed from where she sat cross-legged on the couch, "but she'll get through it. The two of you have managed far worse."

He massaged a hand along the back of his neck. "Why is it that kicking cancer's butt now feels easier than dealing with a posse of not-very-nice little girls?"

"Because you knew what to do to fight cancer. Mean girls are more sinister, even the elementary school version."

"No doubt. I'm proud of her, though. She did the right thing by calling me."

"Are you going to tell the mom?"

He shrugged. When he'd arrived at the house where the sleepover was taking place, his daughter had claimed to have a stomachache. The birthday girl's mother had been solicitous and sympathetic, although it was clear she had wanted him to take Anna away from the party.

He should be used to that. After her cancer, it felt like no one truly trusted that she was well. Every minor cold or stomach bug took on a greater meaning. He'd been the same way at first, and Anna had been the one to remind him that she was fine.

She was healthy.

Yes, they visited the oncologist for regular checkups, and he lost several nights of sleep before each of those visits. But his daughter remained cancer-free. And Josh knew that even if she faced another health crisis, they'd find a way to overcome it. He was committed to that more than anything in his life.

Tonight his daughter hadn't left the party because of any legitimate physical ailment. She'd called him because one of the first activities the girls had decided to engage in was prank phone calls. Instead of the harmless fun he remembered as a kid, they were targeting some of the kids in their class, including Evie.

"Anna doesn't want me to tell. She said that will

make it worse. The girls think she left because she felt sick, just like the mom does."

"But you can't let them get away with bullying other kids, especially Evie."

"I know." Josh raked his hands through his hair. Sweet, gentle Evie was more than Anna's best friend. In a lot of ways, the quiet girl reminded Josh of himself as a kid. He'd allowed himself to be vulnerable, both to his father and to some of the jerks at his school. But he'd had Parker to protect him.

His brother had come out of the womb as an alpha, just like Anna. He wanted to tell his daughter to face down those girls and call them out on their awful behavior. But he knew—even if he didn't understand—that girl problems were different, more complicated. This was when he wished his ex-wife was more a part of Anna's life.

And a reminder of why having the right woman at his side would be good for more than just him.

"I'll call Mara tomorrow and ask for her advice," he said and tried to ignore the flash of disappointment in Ella's gaze. Had she wanted him to ask for her help on figuring this out? That seemed impossible. She'd made it clear she didn't want to be involved in Anna's life, despite doing a great job with his kid in her own weird way.

"Dad?" Anna's soft voice came from the top of the stairs. "Can you come up here for a minute?"

"Sure, sweetheart."

"I've got to run back to my house for something."
Ella stood from the sofa.

"Right now?"

She nodded. "I'll be back in less than a half hour."

"Sure."

It was his turn for disappointment. He needed support at the moment, and she was leaving. It shouldn't surprise or hurt his feelings, but it did.

"Dad!" Anna's voice was more insistent now.

"Coming," he called back and turned away from Ella before he revealed too much.

Ella rubbed two fingers against her chest as she walked up the path to Josh's house twenty minutes later. His comment about going to Mara for advice made sense. She reminded herself of that over and over, but somehow it didn't make it hurt any less.

In a few weeks, when she was out on assignment again, this time wouldn't matter. Her final summer in Starlight would seem like a distant memory, along with Josh and the way he made her feel.

She wouldn't think about him or Anna or wonder what might have been if she was a different person. A better woman. Once she settled into her career and the relentless travel and all that came with it, there would be no time to ruminate over the people she'd left behind.

It would be simple to walk away. Heck, she could do it now if she needed to, even after what they'd shared earlier tonight, which felt like ages ago at this point.

Just as she lifted her hand to knock, the front door opened. "I thought you weren't coming back," Josh said as he frowned at her.

Gone was the personable, easygoing man and in his place, a surly, bristling tortured soul stood in front of her.

"I told you I'd be back."

He gave a tight nod.

"You didn't believe me?"

"Trust issues," he muttered, then sighed. "I'm glad to see you. I missed you."

One corner of her mouth twitched before she could stop it. "I've been gone less than thirty minutes, just like I said."

His strong features softened as he opened the door wider for her. "I still missed you."

Easy to walk away, she repeated to herself. Sure it would be.

"Is Anna still in her room?"

He glanced behind him, then returned his gaze to Ella. "She's watching TV."

"I brought supplies." She patted the duffel bag looped over one shoulder.

"What kind of supplies?"

She winked and edged past him. "You'll see."

She blew out a breath as she moved forward. Was she in any position to offer the comfort she wanted to give? Her heart squeezed as she approached the sullen little girl wrapped in a blanket on the comfy sofa. "How's it going, kid?"

Anna didn't take her eyes off the television. "I really wanted to sleep over."

"I know, but you did the right thing leaving. Fun isn't very fun when it comes at the expense of other people."

"I guess," the girl agreed.

"What do you think about the two of us doing our own spa night?"

Anna shifted, although she looked doubtful. "You don't seem like you know how to do a spa night. Aubrey's mom wears lots of makeup and has really shiny hair."

Ella frowned as she touched a hand to her messy bun. "I appreciate great skin care as well as the next person." She could feel Josh watching her from the doorway to the family room and wondered for a moment what he thought about her hair and typical lack of makeup. Not that it mattered. She didn't take care of herself to impress a man, and her years of traveling had honed her beauty routine to only what was essential.

She should have expected that Anna wasn't going to make an attempt to help easy. But that only made Ella more determined.

She placed her duffel on the coffee table. "In fact, I have products that the little meanie's mom couldn't possibly access because they come from all over the world. I've gone to some amazing places, and I have lotions and potions that smell better than heaven and will make your skin just as soft. Those little jerks will wish they'd been nicer to you and Evie and better people in general."

"You aren't supposed to call someone a name, even if she is a meanie," Anna corrected, but she unwrapped the blanket and scooted to the edge of the seat cushion.

"Which is why we can all agree that I'm a terrible role model." Ella said the words with a laugh even though she didn't find the idea behind them funny. "But I have great skin care products in my bag of tricks."

"What do they smell like?" Anna asked as she leaned toward the bag when Ella started to unzip it.

"Like honey and vanilla," Josh said from the doorway.

Ella's stomach did a little tumble at the fact that he recognized her scent. Like it meant something about how well he knew her. "You know, sometimes when I worked in tiny villages, it would be days before I could shower, so I always made sure I had lotion and soaps that smelled nice. I was close to patients, many of whom were in a lot of pain, and I wanted them to associate me with something good."

Anna reached for one of the jars, a vanilla face scrub Cory had given Ella as a gift for Christmas last year.

As she untwisted the cap, Anna nodded at Ella. "I remember how the hospital smelled when I went for chemo. The waiting room stank like hot dogs sometimes." She grimaced. "I hate hot dogs now."

"I was never a fan," Ella answered.

"But one of the nurses smelled like apples. She was always nice and hugged me and told me I was brave and strong."

Ella swallowed against the lump of emotion rising in her throat. "You are brave and strong."

Anna closed her eyes and inhaled the fragrance of the face scrub. "Not tonight. I should have told those girls that they were being stupid and it isn't nice to do prank calls or make fun of people."

"Sometimes it's hard to know the right words to say at the moment, but you did the right thing by walking away. Evie is lucky to have you as a friend."

"Can we paint our nails, too?" Anna asked, clearly not wanting to revisit the scene from earlier tonight any longer.

Ella smiled. "I have the prettiest polish colors. I went a little crazy when I returned to Starlight. I hadn't done my nails in years and wanted all the options."

"We can go up to Daddy's bathroom," Anna said, hopping off the sofa and placing the jar back in the bag. "He's got more room than me."

"If it's okay with him." Ella turned, but Josh had disappeared from the doorway.

"Daddy!" Anna shouted, cupping her hands around her mouth. "Can me and Ella use your bathroom for our spa night?"

He reappeared and Ella couldn't help but notice that his eyes seemed a little red-rimmed. "Do I get an invitation to spa night?"

"No way," Anna told him. "Girls only."

"That's discrimination," Josh complained with a smile. He kept his focus on his daughter like he couldn't quite meet Ella's gaze. "But I guess I can make snacks. There are always snacks and special drinks at a spa, right?"

Anna beamed. "Probably milkshakes would be best."

"Strawberry," Ella added.

"Strawberry milkshakes coming right up," he agreed.

As Ella followed Anna toward the staircase, Josh put a hand on her arm. "Thank you," he whispered, and something about the look in his eyes made her knees go a little weak.

"Sure," she said and headed up the stairs.

Chapter Twelve

Three days later, Josh watched Ella from the newly constructed front porch of one of the cabins at Tall Pines Camp. She stood like a statue at the end of the dock that jutted out into the lake.

He hadn't talked to her since she'd left his house the previous Saturday night. That evening had been a whirlwind of conflicting emotions—from happiness at having her come apart under him to frustration and anger because of Anna's difficulties at the sleepover to gratitude when Ella had returned to salvage the evening with her impromptu spa night.

She and Anna had spent an hour laughing in his master bath as they slathered on skin care goop and painted each other's nails. He'd been relegated to the task of providing milkshakes and snacks, which suited him fine. Not that he wouldn't don a face mask to make his daughter happy, but he was relieved to have Ella take the reins on lifting Anna's spirits.

Their conversation about the scents of the hospital and memories of Anna's months in chemo had just about gutted him. In truth, he could barely look at a hot dog thanks to the association he had with the scent of the hospital waiting room. Anna had needed cheering up after the party, and he appreciated Ella's willingness to step in. She never seemed to stop surprising him.

It also made him recommitted to finding a woman to add to his and Anna's lives in the long term. Both of them could clearly benefit from a little more female influence, and Ella wasn't someone they could become attached to, despite the ever-growing affection he felt and the way his daughter seemed to connect with her.

They hadn't gotten to the dating apps because Ella had left shortly after her nails dried. He and Anna had watched her favorite princess movie, and he'd thought about inviting Ella to stay. Hell, he owed her more than he could say at this point.

But he didn't ask because he wanted her to stay far too much. Not just for a movie but long term in Starlight.

Hearing her talk about the minute details of her time as a traveling nurse made him realize he had no right to expect anything of her. She was her own person. If she was determined to leave their town behind, who was he to stop her?

He was a fool for letting his heart get involved.

As he watched, Ella lifted her hands outstretched on either side of her like she was a bird about to take flight. And then she did, diving into the lake fully clothed.

Or maybe she'd fallen?

Josh didn't give himself time to think. He hustled off the porch toward the lake, his footfalls thundering down the dock.

He shouted her name, and by the time he got to the end of the dock, he breathed a sigh of relief as he saw her head pop up out of the water a few feet away. Sunlight glinted off the water and he squinted as he stared at Ella, trying to determine what the heck possessed her to jump into the lake.

"Are you okay?" he demanded.

She slicked her hair back from her face and let out a joyful cackle. "You should come in," she said, beckoning to him. "The water is amazing."

He dropped to his knees and reached down a hand to dip his fingers into the lake. "It's freezing."

"So refreshing. Good for the soul."

"Your soul needs a reality check."

She shook her head and reclined back to float on top of the water. The T-shirt she wore had become transparent, and he could see the outline of the red lace bra under the pale yellow fabric.

"I've dealt with reality for far too long," she countered. "I wanted a reprieve for a moment. Those few seconds in the air, I was weightless and free."

He stared at her for a long moment, then looked over his shoulder. No one was around. He knew the campers had gone on a nature hike this morning with the counseling staff. Kayla and Rob had driven into town to pick up a load of lumber at the hardware store.

He had a lot more work to finish today and did not have a change of clothes in his truck, but despite his better sense, he toed off his boots, tossed his wallet onto the dock and catapulted himself into the water.

"Cannonball," he yelled and had the satisfaction of hearing Ella laugh again before he went under. He surfaced with a gasp.

The water was even colder than he anticipated, but those first seconds and the shock of it had also managed to wash away a lot of his worries and frustrations.

"Look at you being all adventurous. I wish I had a camera now and I'd take a picture of you. This would be the perfect setup to show your fun and fancy-free side on a dating app."

Her determination to set him up with another woman dampened his joy for a moment, but he recovered. He felt too good and alive, and despite Ella's single-minded focus on finding a woman for him, he attributed much of that to her.

Without thinking about the repercussions, he swam the remaining distance between them and wrapped his arms around her as they treaded water. He fused his mouth to hers and hoped she could understand everything he wasn't able to say out loud through the kiss.

Goose bumps erupted along his body that had nothing to do with the temperature of the water. It was nearly ten in the morning, and the air was already warm thanks to the bright summer sun. But the heat inside him had everything to do with Ella. She moaned and opened for him, and he quickly lost himself in her.

"You're getting good at practicing," she said against his jaw.

He thought about responding with a teasing snippet—something along the lines of practice making perfect. In that case, he was ready to spend the next several weeks practicing with Ella, but he didn't say anything.

Instead, he kissed her again, slowly, tenderly. He didn't want to remind either of them that this didn't mean anything. He didn't want to think about her leaving or about dating some infinitely appropriate woman even though that was what he needed to do. It was what Ella expected and wanted.

If he stayed in the moment, the future wouldn't matter. He'd become a bit of an expert at that.

When his ex-wife had left him at the tail end of Anna's cancer treatments, staying in the moment had helped him survive the pain and the fear of taking care of his daughter on his own.

But pain and fear were no way to live.

A shiver ran through Ella, and he pulled her closer.

"Okay, adventure woman. I think it's time to get you dried off. Me, too, for that matter."

She nodded, and he noticed her lips were turning an alarming shade of blue.

"Seriously, Ella. The water isn't that cold. Anna said they were planning a swim day at the end of the week."

"I'm sensitive," she said as she pushed away from him. "Don't make fun of me for it."

She paddled toward the dock and he followed.

"I'm not making fun, sweetheart. But I am thinking about the quickest way to get you warm." As she exited the water by climbing the ladder attached to the side of the dock, he reached up and hefted himself onto the edge of the wooden planks.

"When do you think Kayla and Rob will be back?" she asked as she turned on her back and looked up at the cloudless sky. Her chest rose and fell in shallow puffs of breath.

He stood and straddled her denim-clad legs. "I'm not sure, but we have enough time to get you fully heated. I can work fast when I set my mind to it."

She took the hand he offered and then shivered again. "Then let's get going before my extremities freeze off."

He squeezed her fingers, then picked up his boots and shoved his wallet back into his pocket. They ran together down the dock and up the hill to the empty cabin. "I can hear your teeth chattering," he said. "Ella, it's seventy degrees out."

"Sensitive," she repeated like a challenge. He slammed shut the door on the cabin and smoothed his hands over her face.

"Good to know," he told her as he lifted the wet shirt up and over her head. He was definitely up for the challenge.

They stripped down with as much efficiency as they could manage with wet clothes that clung to them like a second skin. Plucking the condom packet from his wallet, he led her to the cabin's small bathroom, where he flipped on the water, adjusting the temperature to nearly scalding.

"We can't use the shower," she said. "Kayla will know—"

"No one is going to know except you and me," he told her. "This is just about you and me, Ella."

She bit down on her lower lip and a groan erupted from his throat, but she didn't argue. Once the steam filled the small space, he opened the sliding door and followed her in, kissing her as the water sluiced over them.

It only took a few minutes before the trembling subsided and she was warm and pliant and perfect in his arms. It took a little creativity to figure out how to manage their coupling in the tiny shower, but Josh appreciated the chance to be creative with this woman.

She practically melted in his arms and he held her as they both regained their breath. For a long while, they stood together under the spray of a hot shower... at least until the water began to turn cold.

While she dried off, Josh threw their clothes in the dryer, then grabbed a blanket from the cabin's bunk room. He wrapped it around her shoulders and carried her to the porch while they waited for the dryer cycle to finish.

She laughed even as she rested her head on his shoulder. "You know I can walk? I'm not cold anymore."

"I have no doubt you can do whatever you set your mind to," he told her. "This is me using any excuse to keep my hands on you."

"I can respect that." She kissed his jaw. "I like having an adventure with you."

"You and me both." Josh wanted to have more. He wanted to make plans for the future, but he didn't dare. Being adventurous might be okay for him but acting with reckless abandon when his daughter would also be affected was something different. A chance that Josh wouldn't take, even for a woman who made him feel the way Ella did.

They sat on the porch together looking out at the camp, neither of them speaking. He didn't know for sure but got the impression she was as unwilling to let reality intrude on this moment as him.

When the dryer buzzer sounded, he went and retrieved their clothes.

"This was a great adventure," he said against her lips as he kissed her once again.

"Very great," Ella agreed with a saucy smile before he watched her walk away toward the camp's main cabin.

He had plenty of work to keep him busy but sat down on one of the Adirondack chairs, bent forward to place his head in his hands and silently wondered how he was going to find a woman who made him feel the way Ella did. A woman who would help him forget this unexpected summer fling that was coming to mean everything to him.

Ella walked next to her sister-in-law through the weekend farmers market hosted in the Dennison Mill parking lot.

"I wish I were creative and crafty," Kaitlyn said as they took in the booths of handcrafted food, local produce and gifts made by artisans from around the area. "I can't even keep a houseplant alive."

"When I was little, I had a pet rock," Ella shared. "I left him in a pocket and sent him through the washing machine. If you think killing a houseplant is bad, imagine the guilt over letting a rock die."

Kaitlyn chuckled. "I don't think a rock can die."

"His googly eyes fell off. It was akin to murder."

"Well, you overcame any early homicidal tendencies because you became a nurse."

It was a simple factual statement but hit Ella with the force of a knockout punch. Was her career choice enough to make up for all the unfortunate choices she'd made in life?

She cleared her throat and forced a smile. "Cory could teach you some stuff about jewelry making," she suggested. Her friend had started making jewelry when she'd first arrived in Starlight and was quickly growing a cult following of fans in the area. "In fact, we've got to stop by her booth tonight. I have a friend who lives in San Francisco with a milestone birthday coming up. I want to send her a pair of earrings and a matching bracelet as a gift."

"Cory is certainly talented," Kaitlyn agreed. "But I'm not sure I have anything to learn from her. I'm more a consumer than a maker."

Ella nodded. "Me, too."

"You're branching out in the cooking club. That takes creativity."

"But am I retaining any of the lessons?" Ella asked with a laugh. "And if you tell Madison I admitted that, I will deny it and then make her believe that you criticized her green chili recipe."

"I would never." Kaitlyn held up her hands. "Madison's cooking is perfect. You've made some great friends in Starlight, El. It makes Finn happy to see you surrounded by people who support you. He told me about the friction at dinner the other night."

Ella felt her shoulders grow tense. She loved her sister-in-law and appreciated the gentling effect Kaitlyn had on Finn, but she wasn't exactly interested in dissecting her family dynamics with anyone.

"It was fine. No big deal. I wonder whether the goat milk soap people are here. I love that stuff."

Kaitlyn placed a hand on Ella's arm. "I know your dad isn't perfect. He made a lot of mistakes after your mom died, but he's changed. I saw that first-hand working for him."

"Working for him and being his daughter are two different things," Ella snapped, then regretted it. Kaitlyn meant well. She knew that. Plus, Ella didn't have too much more time in Starlight. There was no reason to leave town with bad blood between them. "Honestly, I think my dad and I are fine."

Kaitlyn let out a delicate snort that she tried to cover with a cough. "Just like that rock of yours was fine after the spin cycle."

Ella rolled her eyes, then laughed when Kaitlyn grinned. "You're older than me," she pointed out. "That should equate to being more mature. And married, which means you're supposed to be both more settled and wiser."

"I don't think that's in a rule book."

"It should be."

"I'll keep it in mind. Did you know your dad is driving to Seattle next week to have his biannual blood work done?"

Ella sucked in a breath. "I didn't know that, but I'm sure he'll be fine."

Kaitlyn nodded, then waved to someone across the parking lot before returning her attention to Ella. "I'm sure he will, too. Normally Finn or I go with him to these big appointments, but we have an appointment here that Jack refuses to let me reschedule."

"A doctor's appointment?" Ella didn't want to think about another person close to her having health issues, even her father now that he'd beaten cancer. A nurse who was bothered to be around sick people wasn't much help to anyone, but things in Starlight were too personal to deal with in any sort of rational way.

Kaitlyn tried her best to look casual, but it didn't quite work. "I've had some issues over the years with endometriosis. We're thinking about starting a family, and the doctor wants me to come in for some initial testing. I'm sure it's not a big deal. Everything will be fine."

Ella immediately reached out to hug Kaitlyn. "It will be fine. If you and my brother want to start a family, nothing will stop you. I have complete faith in Finn's stubbornness to see you through."

To her great relief, Kaitlyn's features seemed to relax at that. "I want this so much," she whispered.

"Then you'll have it," Ella told her. She had no right to make that kind of a promise. There was no guarantee of anything. During her last few months as a traveling nurse, before she returned to Starlight, hope had become one of the things she hated the most.

There were times when she knew nothing would save one of her young patients, but the mothers inevitably held out hope until the last moment when an unthinkable loss crushed their hearts and souls.

She'd done her best to be caring and sympathetic without giving false hope. Several of her colleagues had chided her for that. But Ella felt like she was doing people a service.

Why would she add to their eventual pain and suffering by making them believe in a future that wasn't going to come true? Happy endings were few and far between in the places she worked and with the population she served. But she'd be damned if she was going to dash Kaitlyn's hopes.

They continued to walk through the farmers market, each buying several items from local crafters. Finn caught up with them as Kaitlyn was choosing vegetables from a farm stand.

"I don't know why she can't let me exist on SpaghettiOs and ramen," he told Ella after hugging his wife.

"Because I love you," Kaitlyn said and blew a lock of blond hair away from her face.

"Hey, Ella and I turned out okay on a steady diet of processed foods."

"Only after Mom died," she reminded him. "She was an excellent cook."

"Do you have any of her recipes saved?" Kaitlyn asked.

Ella shook her head. "I'm not sure. There might be something at Dad's house."

"I can ask him." Kaitlyn nodded.

"I'll talk to him about it," Ella offered.

She didn't miss the look that Kaitlyn and Finn shared.

"We're talking about recipes," she reminded her brother. "Dad and I can certainly get along for that conversation."

"It's not you that I'm worried about. Dad wants to make things better, and you seem intent on crushing him."

"So I should give him a do-over on all the ways he treated me badly in the past?"

"I don't think *do-over* is the right word. But maybe a fresh start going forward wouldn't be out of the question?"

He was right. She could admit that now, but it still felt wrong. She worried that if she accepted her dad into her life and heart, she would be letting him off the hook for the way he'd hurt and emotionally abandoned her when she needed him the most.

"I can't promise anything." She shrugged. "But I'll find Mom's recipes if he still has them."

Finn looked like he wanted to argue, but Kaitlyn took his hand and squeezed.

"I'm gonna head out," Ella told the two of them.

"Are you sure?" Kaitlyn asked gently. "Mara and Parker are hosting everyone at their house for s'mores after the market."

Everyone would include Josh and Anna. As much as Ella wanted to see them both, she nodded. "It's been a long day. I'll talk to you guys later. And Finn…" She cleared her throat.

Her brother cocked an eyebrow.

"As annoying as you are as a brother, you're going to make a great dad one day." She had the satisfaction of leaving her brother speechless, which didn't happen very often.

As she walked away, Ella caught sight of Josh standing with Parker at the far end of the aisle.

Her gaze caught on his, and he smiled.

She didn't return it but turned and quickly headed for her car. She understood she was being rude and immature, but every time they were together he managed to crash through more of her defenses. Ella didn't like it.

Things were getting too real for her in Starlight. As tempted as she was to change her plans and stay, another part of her knew leaving at the end of the summer was the only way to keep her heart safe. That moment couldn't come fast enough.

Chapter Thirteen

Josh waited outside Main Street Perk the following Tuesday morning. He took a moment to admire the charming storefronts that lined each side of the street. Starlight was beautiful in the summer, so bright and shiny and alive with promise.

"The planter boxes are amazing," a soft voice said next to him. He turned to see a pretty woman who looked to be around his age smiling at him.

"I wish the ones on my front porch looked half as good," he agreed and then silently berated himself. Was it cool or überdorky for a man to admit he cared about flower boxes?

"You're Josh?"

He nodded.

"I'm Crystal, Mara's friend."

"It's nice to meet you, Crystal." He'd almost said no when his sister-in-law had suggested he meet one of the vendors from the farmers market for a date.

The longer he went down this path, the less enthusiastic he felt about spending time with any woman other than Ella. He'd eventually agreed after she'd blown him off at the farmers market.

It wasn't as if he didn't know the score of their relationship. But his heart refused to believe she didn't feel the same way he did. Maybe he was confusing great sex for something more. Something it didn't mean, at least not to her.

"I'm glad this worked," he said.

Her smile was open and without any of the skepticism he often saw in Ella's eyes.

He was a sucker for a challenge, but he blamed that on his childhood and all the time he'd spent trying to think of a way to get his dad's attention or respect.

Despite failing over and over, he'd never given up and didn't necessarily like what that said about him. "I have to tell you, I'm not usually a fan of candles, but Mara gave me one of yours. My house has never smelled better."

Crystal looked pleased by the compliment. She was a pretty woman, petite and blonde with a fresh face and her long hair pulled back into a heavy braid. So what if his stomach didn't do backflips when he looked at her? The backflips might come eventually.

They stepped inside and ordered coffee and muffins. Nanci, the shop's owner, gave him a not-so-subtle thumbs-up as they headed toward a table near the far wall. Each black café table had a mason jar of fresh flowers in the middle, and the walls were painted a sunny yellow. Josh tried to let the cheery interior bolster his flagging mood. He had no reason to be grumpy and did his best to hide it from Crystal.

She was kind, funny and easy to talk to. She'd grown up in a small town in western Idaho that she'd left at the urging of her now ex-boyfriend.

Josh didn't share the details of his history the way he had with Ella, but it wasn't difficult to talk to her about his life in Starlight with Anna.

Crystal had three sisters, a brother, plus a bevy of nieces and nephews, so she seemed happy to hear about his daughter.

It was probably a huge first-date faux pas to talk about his child with a woman who didn't have a history with her, but Josh figured if a woman couldn't take his daughter being a big part of his life, then she definitely wasn't the woman for him.

Crystal had no problem with it, and Josh hated himself for trying to find something wrong with her, any excuse not to like her or ask her on a second date.

The truth was she seemed perfect in all the ways that counted, and they arranged to go out to dinner Saturday night. He certainly wasn't at the point where he'd introduce her to Anna, but this date was the positive start he thought he wanted. The one he'd been sure he wanted before his feelings for Ella changed things.

They got up, and after depositing their trash and saying goodbye to Nanci and Mara, he started toward the door only to have the woman who consumed most of his waking and—if he was honest—dream-time thoughts walk into the coffee shop.

Was he imagining the hush that fell over the patrons as their gazes met?

Ella's gaze tracked over Crystal and then back to Josh. She nodded a greeting, but her eyes had gone blank as if they were a couple of casual acquaintances running into each other.

As if he didn't know the sweet noises she made as she came apart in his arms or the way she sometimes snorted when she laughed too hard. He wasn't sure of the appropriate next step. Did he introduce the woman he might start dating to the woman with whom he was currently sleeping? That seemed out of the question.

In her decisive way, Ella answered for him by turning and walking toward the counter.

If Crystal noticed the tension between the two of them, she was polite enough to ignore it. He escorted her to her car, gave her an awkward hug and watched her drive away with a wave.

His truck was parked a couple of spaces away at the curb in front of Trophy Room. Instead of heading in that direction, he returned to the coffee shop.

He ducked into the shadowed alley between

two buildings and tried not to think of himself as a stalker. He and Ella needed to talk. They were friends, and he didn't appreciate the way she was treating him.

Her stride was purposeful as she walked past, and he stepped out and called her name.

She turned, her mouth filled with a bite of the bear claw she held in one hand.

"Why are you avoiding me?" he demanded. "I thought you'd be first in line to offer words of encouragement."

She stared at him while she chewed, then swallowed and shrugged. "For what? Going on a date with the most vanilla woman you could find? Way to go. Hope you guys are happy together."

A flake of glazed sugar clung to the corner of her mouth, and Josh had the urge to close the distance between them and lick it away.

"You don't even know her."

Ella shoved the pastry into the brown bag she carried along with it. "I know plenty just from seeing her. There's no reason to get your boxers in a bunch. I approve. If Mara had run the idea past me, I would have said the two of you would make a perfect couple. Vanilla suits you."

"I guess so," he agreed, even though he wanted to argue. Hers was the only kind of vanilla he cared for. He wanted her to admit she was lying. Ella suited him, but he wasn't going to admit that when she was so determined to be contrary.

"I guess I didn't need a dating app after all." He took a step closer. "It's a good thing because we got a little distracted the other night before we could discuss my options there."

"Won't happen again," she promised. She was smarter than him. They should stop what was developing between them before the freight train of feeling took over.

"I still appreciate everything you've done for Anna and me," he said, trying not to sound like an imbecile. Fairly certain he failed. "Who knows what will happen with Crystal, but that doesn't have to change the two of us being friends."

Something he couldn't quite define flashed in her blue eyes. It looked like disappointment or regret. Either way, it hurt his heart to see it. The last thing he wanted was to cause her pain.

"We are friends," she agreed, and the words seemed to surprise her as much as they did him. "I hope things work out with this new person. You should be happy."

"Thanks," he muttered and ran a hand through his hair. He didn't want to talk to Ella about another woman, even though that was the whole basis of their relationship. "We've only had coffee. There's no guarantee anything more will come of it."

"I'm sure if Mara approves then it's all good."

"Maybe," he agreed, trying to think of something better to say. Words that would bridge the distance between them but still keep his heart protected. "Are you heading out to camp?"

She gave him an almost embarrassed smile. "I'm filling in at Dr. Anderson's office today."

"That's Anna's pediatrician."

"A lot of kids in town see him," Ella said with a nod. "He's been around since Finn and I were little."

"What are you doing for him?"

She shrugged. "His nurse has a daughter who's about to give birth. She wants to be there so he asked if I'd work a few shifts. He heard that I was helping out at Tall Pines."

A feather could have knocked Josh over at that news. "And you agreed?"

"There's no need to look so surprised. I can be helpful when I set my mind to it. Maybe I'm giving you a run for your money as the go-to gal for people in this town. Not that you're a gal because you're the go-to guy. I'd be the gal." She fluttered her fingers between them as if to clarify that he was a man and she was a woman.

"I understood what you meant. Does this new-found interest in making yourself invaluable around town mean you might be thinking of staying?"

She didn't answer for several seconds, and Josh realized he was holding his breath. He wanted her to say yes. If she said yes, that could potentially change everything. If she said yes, they might actually be able to make something real of their relationship.

"I made a commitment to Traveling Nurses. The plan remains the same."

He did his best to hide his disappointment. "Of course it does."

"I'll be back at camp on Friday for game day."

Friday was the final day of the current camp session, and they celebrated each ending with team activities and games, inviting the parents to join their kids.

"I'll see you there," he said.

Then before she could walk away, he reached out and touched a finger to her lip. "A crumb," he explained.

She swiped her hand over her mouth. "I like those bear claws way too much."

He smiled. "Me, too. Way more than a regular vanilla glazed doughnut. Just for the record."

She rolled her eyes. "I've told you before, Johnson. Your lame attempts at charm are lost on me." Then she turned and headed down the sidewalk.

And no matter how much the urge to follow her roared through him, Josh ignored it.

As Ella stood near the shoreline of the Tall Pines lake Friday afternoon, she couldn't help but think of the swim she and Josh had taken together and what had come after.

It seemed like a lifetime ago that he'd wrapped his arms around her and warmed her body one blissful inch at a time. During her career, she'd traveled around the world and learned plenty about staying in the moment. Clearly not enough. Now all she could think about was the recent past and how she hadn't appreciated it enough when she was part of it.

Spending time with Josh and Anna seemed so effortless, but now she wished she'd let them know how much they meant to her. Because after the conversation with him outside of Main Street Perk, it felt as though things had shifted again and not in a way she liked.

She'd stayed in the nurse's office for most of the morning as the kids participated in various team activities. Most of the parents had arrived for the burgers Kayla and Rob were grilling as part of the end-of-camp celebration.

A new camp session with a different theme would start on Monday. Many of the same kids were signed up, but a few would say goodbye at the end of the day.

Ella hated saying goodbye, although she should be a pro because she'd done it enough over the years. In her time helping out around the property and then in the nurse's role, she'd gotten to know many of the kids. Despite her best efforts, she liked them. She felt close to them. She would miss them when they were gone.

Once she made it to the picnic area, several parents introduced themselves, and she recognized a couple from around town.

Strange to think that people she'd graduated high school with had children old enough to attend a summer camp. She couldn't imagine the maturity and responsibility it would take to be a parent.

Although she was more than ready to be a doting aunt to Finn and Kaitlyn's baby whenever they had one.

Anna and Evie came running up to her, both wrapped in colorful beach towels. The girls had wet hair and knobby knees sticking out from the towels and looked blissfully happy the way kids should.

"That water is freezing," Evie said.

"It's not so bad." Anna nudged her friend. "You get used to it."

Evie wrapped the fluffy towel more closely around herself. "I didn't get used to it."

"Me neither," Ella agreed.

"She's sensitive," a deep voice said from behind her.

Awareness zinged across her nerve endings like she'd taken a straight shot of adrenaline to the heart.

"You'll get warm now that you're here in the sun," she told Evie. She did her best to ignore Josh, which was hard when he came to stand next to her, their shoulders practically touching. Difficult, not hard. She wasn't going to associate the word *hard* with Josh.

Too bad her body refused to cooperate.

"Daddy needs your help tomorrow night," Anna announced. "That's why we were coming to talk to you."

"And here I thought you just enjoyed the pleasure of my company."

"We like you, too." Evie nodded, then yelped as Anna reached out to pinch her. "It's okay to like her, Anna."

"I know." Anna rolled her big chocolate eyes. "But I don't because she's—"

"It's fine, girls," Josh interrupted before Anna could finish sharing what she thought about Ella. Probably a blessing for Ella. "I told you we'll figure it out."

Ella glanced at Josh out of the corner of her eye. "Can't decide on the appropriate wardrobe choices for your big date?" She gave him an exaggerated once-over. "I highly recommend shirts that don't look like you've been wearing them for the past month."

"He has more shirts than you'd think." Anna rubbed a hand over her nose. "He buys like ten of the same color so he doesn't have to think about what he's wearing."

"I'm color-blind," Josh said. "It's not nice to make fun of people who struggle." He reached out a finger and tapped it against his daughter's nose. "I'm lucky I have you to help me shop."

Now Ella felt horrible for saying anything about his clothes. "I didn't know," she said. "I'm sorry."

He grinned. "It's fine. I'm not bothered by it anymore. Parker used to have fun messing with me."

"You should yell at me or tell me I'm a horrible person," she continued. "I can't even make a joke without it legitimately offending someone."

"You didn't offend me, Ella."

He looked like he wanted to reach for her. Oh, how Ella wanted that as well. But he didn't move. He might have shifted away from her, almost imperceptibly, but she noticed.

Anna stepped forward. "You can make it up to him by babysitting me tomorrow night so he can go on a date."

"She was supposed to stay with me," Evie explained. "But Mommy and Parker and me are going camping."

"Daddy, when are we going to go camping?" Anna asked before turning back to Ella. "Will you stay with me?"

A pained look flashed in Josh's dark eyes. "Anna, I've got calls out to a few potential sitters. We'll find—"

"Sure, I'll babysit." Ella was proud of how level her voice sounded. Like this wasn't making her heart want to shrivel up inside her chest. "My pleasure."

"Awesome. I told him to ask you," Anna said, turning to Evie. "Ella is even more determined than me to find Daddy a girlfriend."

"Let's go get something to eat," Evie told Anna. "I'm starving."

Anna grabbed her hand, and the two girls ran off toward the picnic tables.

"I can pay a sitter to stay with her," Josh said when they were gone.

His voice was low and disgruntled, which Ella had to admit she liked more than his easy affability. She took a moment to compose herself before turning to him with her best saucy smile. "Who says I'm not charging you?"

"Ella."

"What time, Josh?"

He scrubbed a hand over his face and the sound of his bristling stubble made her weak in the knees. She hated her knees.

"I bought tickets to an outdoor concert over in Fairplay. I planned to take Crystal to dinner and then to the show, so it might be a late night. I can—"

She felt the edges of her smile turn brittle, but it held, which was what counted. "What time?"

"Would six work?" he asked with a sigh.

"Perfect."

"Ella, I don't want—"

"This is what we both wanted, Josh. It's all good. I hope you have an amazing time." She pretended to wave to someone past his shoulder. "I've got to go. I'll see you tomorrow. And Josh?"

"Yes?"

"Whatever you wear will be perfect because that's just how you are."

He laughed softly. "Thanks. You're a great dating coach, Ella."

"Yep," she agreed and walked away before the tears that stung the back of her throat made their way into her eyes.

Chapter Fourteen

"No, no, no." Ella raced toward the child who dangled from a cliff on the side of the Brazilian mountain range. "Don't let go," she yelled.

The young boy's mother's scream reverberated through the verdant valley. The peaks that surrounded them looked like jagged shark teeth ready to attack. Ella concentrated on placing one foot in front of the other as she ran over the rocky terrain. A trip and fall and then up again and pounding forward, ignoring the scrapes on her knees and the sting from her bloody palms.

"Hold on," she shouted. The child met her gaze, his night-sky eyes dark and pained.

To her horror, he released one hand from where it

clung to the rock face and then the other, and before she could reach him, he disappeared, plummeting into the mist below.

Ella woke with a gasp, straightening from the sofa as realization dawned on her that the horrible scene had been nothing but a dream.

And she wasn't alone.

Josh held her shoulders, his gaze intense as he studied her face. "You're okay," he said, although it had to be clear that she wasn't.

She focused on drawing air in and out of her lungs, embarrassed to have been discovered in the throes of one of the nightmares that had plagued her since she'd returned to Starlight. No one, not her father or brother or closest friends, knew about the dreams.

Now Josh did, and she hated the weakness it revealed.

Not enough that she wouldn't take the comfort he offered. She buried her head in the crook of his neck when his arms wrapped around her. He smelled like soap and man, and his big hand tracing circles on her back was the best thing she'd ever felt.

He continued to murmur words of comfort until she started to believe she might be okay. But only here, in the moment, with this man who didn't belong to her. Her heart demanded she allow herself to enjoy the solace his embrace provided, if only for a few more minutes.

It sometimes took hours for the adrenaline to fade

after one of her vivid dreams. With Josh holding her, she was able to come back to herself in minutes.

The air between them grew heavy and charged, and she began to notice more than the comforting scent of him. She felt the muscles on his arms bunch when she shifted her hands to squeeze them. His broad shoulders seemed to engulf her, and she could feel the strength of him—the hard wall of his chest against her body.

Heat radiated from him, and as he whispered his sweet words, his breath tickled her neck and earlobe.

She wanted to reach up and draw his mouth to hers. At this moment, she wanted to forget the dream and remember the pleasure of their bodies joining together.

Instead, she pulled away, drawing up her knees in front of her like some sort of toll bridge he couldn't cross.

He moved his hand to her ankle, respecting her need for a bit of physical distance while unwilling to fully release her.

She didn't want him to let her go.

"How was the date?" she forced herself to ask.

He frowned. "Tell me about your nightmare, and I'll tell you about the date."

"Not quite the same thing," she answered with a snort.

"Still…" He smoothed a stray lock of hair away from her face. "Does that happen often?"

"No." She shook her head. "At least not like it used

to be when I first came home. It's silly. Dreams don't mean anything."

"Freud would beg to differ. Is it the same every time?"

"I like to mix it up. Sometimes it's a child about to fall from a cliff. In others, there's a flood that wipes out an entire village I can't save. At first, I had this awful nightmare where I was pointing a gun at one of my patients." She blew out a breath. "As if that would ever happen."

"Have you talked to someone?" His voice was so gentle. She wondered what she'd done to deserve his caring about her at this level. Nothing as far as she could see.

"I don't want to talk. Normally, I'm just relieved to wake up."

"Are you worried about what will happen when you're on assignment again?"

"No," she lied. "This is part of the deal. I had a rough year before I left. A lot of the work I do is vaccination clinics and routine care. But there was a string of patients with more serious conditions. We lost several in a row to infection in one of the towns in South America. After that, they sent me to central Africa, and it wasn't much better. I started to take things too personally."

"Understandable," he murmured.

"No." She drew her knees closer to her body and tried not to think of how many nights she'd wound up in the fetal position as the faces of her young patients darted through her mind. "To do my job, I have to be able to separate my emotions from the care I'm giving. I'm not effective otherwise."

"You're also human, which means you're going to have feelings about certain things, and losing a patient has to be one of the worst things a health-care professional can experience."

She bit down on the inside of her cheek to keep herself from responding. Rehashing the past would only lead to more vulnerability, and Ella couldn't handle that.

"I had bad dreams for a while after Anna was diagnosed, and more so when she ended treatment. It was like my brain couldn't accept what the doctors told us about her recovery so continued to invent the worst-case scenarios. I could control the thoughts during the day but at night—"

"The bad things took over." Ella nodded. "One of the doctors I worked with prescribed sleeping pills, but I didn't want to take them. Without something on board, I couldn't sleep more than a couple of hours at night. It took a toll and finally my boss suggested I needed a break."

"Your boss?"

She looked down at her hands, realizing that she'd revealed more than she meant to. "Yeah. I told everyone the sabbatical was my decision, but I was pretty much forced to take time off. But seriously, enough about me. I'm fine, Josh. Truly I am."

"You didn't seem fine, Ella. Is it a good idea for

you to go back to the job if you're still having night-mares?"

"They've been better recently. Much better. But I saw Kaitlyn at the farmers market, and she told me that my dad is having his blood work run next week in Seattle. I think that was a trigger."

"Do you have reason to think the cancer has re-turned?"

She shook her head. "No, but it still dredged up a lot of emotions. I might not get along with him, but he's family. I love him, even if we don't like each other very much. I don't want to think of somebody in my life possibly having major health issues. It's hard to imagine losing anyone else I care about."

"Is that why you acted the way you did with Anna at the start? She's also a trigger for you."

"That's giving your kid a lot of credit." Ella forced her shoulders away from her ears and tried to ap-pear relaxed.

That was the reason she'd wanted to keep her dis-tance with Anna and Josh, but it felt petty to admit that.

"Don't keep me in suspense. How was the date?"

He moved to the other side of the couch and tipped his head up to stare at the room's white ceiling.

"It was great. We had dinner at a great Italian place, and the food was amazing. The band gave a solid performance, so altogether I couldn't have asked for anything more."

Ella feigned a yawn. "I'm not asking about what

songs you sang along to. I'm asking about the girl. Are you going to make her the star of your sappiest country ballad?"

"Ask Anna. I can't carry a tune."

"Stop being exasperating. Do you like her?"

"Yeah, I like her."

Ella refused to let the pain she felt at his words take hold in her chest.

"Did you kiss her?" She tried to sound teasing but wasn't sure she managed it.

"No." Josh rubbed the heels of his hands against each eye. "I didn't kiss her."

"I understand a sense of gentlemanly respect and honor but—"

"I didn't kiss her because I'm not done kissing you. Or at least I don't want to be. I'm not going to lead her on, although I already feel like I might be doing just that."

"You're not. She seems perfect for you. We both know I'm not perfect in any way."

"I would beg to differ, but assuming you are correct, what if I don't want perfect?"

"It's what you deserve." She unfolded her legs and stood. "You've had plenty of practice, Mr. Johnson. It's time to put those skills I helped you with to good use."

He groaned. "That sounds nearly diabolical."

"It's the right thing for both of us. We're friends, Josh. But bad dreams or no, I'm leaving. There's no point in either of us pretending this can go anywhere. Think of me as your rebound after the divorce."

"I think there's a statute of limitations on a rebound."

"I refuse to believe that. But I know that the sooner you put yourself out there, the sooner you'll find love again. We both know it's not going to be with me."

Ella's heart knew no such thing, but she said the words with as much conviction as she could muster.

After a moment, Josh nodded, and Ella walked out into the dark night alone.

Josh sat in his truck and stared at the building that housed his brother's law firm. Parker had taken over shortly after returning to Starlight. He'd bought out the practice from one of the longtime attorneys in town. The older lawyer still came in on a part-time basis but was mainly retired.

Flicking a glance at the clock on the dashboard, Josh turned off the ignition and then rested his head against the steering wheel, sorely tempted to start banging it. He had approximately one minute until the meeting with Parker and the California construction company representatives was scheduled to begin.

He knew he should be in there now but couldn't bring himself to move. A knock on the window startled him. He turned to see Rudy Marshall, the partially-retired attorney in question, smiling at him.

Josh forced himself to climb out of the vehicle, acting like he'd meant to do it all along.

"Hope I'm not interrupting," Rudy said in his jovial voice.

Rudy was the same age as Josh's father and had been a contemporary of Mac Johnson, serving on town council during Mac's tenure as mayor.

"Just checking email before I head in," Josh lied.

Rudy nodded. "How are you doing, son? I get to spend plenty of time with your brother these days, but I haven't seen much of you around."

"I've been busy." At least that wasn't a lie.

"Succeeding where your old man failed." Rudy clapped a hand on Josh's shoulder.

Josh blinked. "That not quite how things are." It certainly didn't feel that way. "Parker can take a lot of credit for the success of the mill. He was the one to help me turn things around. There's a good chance I would have defaulted on the loan without him."

"Give yourself more credit." Rudy smiled. "The vision for that space was all yours. I know how much energy and effort you put into making it happen."

Rudy had paused on the sidewalk before reaching the door to the law office, so Josh felt compelled to halt his progress as well. But he didn't want to hash through his history or motivations with anyone, especially a guy he knew to be a friend of his late father's.

"It's not a big deal. It was the right time for something like that in town."

"I'll tell you one thing…" Rudy chuckled. "You

didn't get your sense of being humble from your father. Mac would have been crowing to anybody who'd listen about his success. That's why his failure to save the mill was such a thorn in his side. For a while, it was all people around here could talk about."

Josh nodded and kept his features neutral, but a metallic taste infiltrated his mouth, and he felt like his throat was lined with razor blades as he tried to take a steady breath.

He was well aware of his father's frustration at not convincing the mill owners to keep the facility open. Mac had managed to put on a positive face around town, but all bets were off in their house.

Mac's temper was legendary behind closed doors, and his preferred method of blowing off steam was to terrorize his family. Thoughts of his dad had led Josh to buy the mill property in the first place—a bit of a whim in retrospect.

All of those memories had plagued him, and he'd wanted a new association with the piece of Starlight that was such a strange and awful part of his childhood.

He'd ended up in over his head, mostly because he'd still been a mess from the fallout of emotions around his daughter's cancer and his wife leaving. He'd eventually pulled himself together and, along with help from his brother and Mara, had opened the multiuse shopping and restaurant hub to great success. That had led to more work on multiuse spaces around the region, which had led to interest from the California firm.

"I've got to get to the meeting," he told Rudy, inclining his jaw toward the office.

"Of course," the gray-haired man agreed. "I would tell you that your father would be proud of what you've accomplished but we both know Mac didn't like anybody other than himself succeeding. I was happy to see your mother thrive after he was gone. Parker, too, in his own way, although it took him a minute to figure himself out."

Josh's hand was on the vintage doorknob, but Rudy wasn't quite finished with this trip down memory lane. "You were the one I worried about the most."

Josh's stomach clenched. "I'm not the same weak kid I was back then."

Rudy shook his head. "I'm not talking about any weakness. There aren't a lot of people who understood who Mac Johnson truly was, but I did. Believe me, I tried to intervene, but your mother wouldn't have it."

Josh nodded. His mom had done her best to protect her sons from the worst of her husband's rage, but she'd hid her bruises and fear. She'd been convinced no one would believe her or step in to help and that speaking out against Mac would only make things worse.

Maybe she'd been right about that. Despite doing his best not to focus on the past, Josh wished she'd tried to get them out of the situation. He wondered what would have happened if they'd had an early chance at a new start.

"It took a special kind of strength to survive him. Strength I don't think you ever gave yourself credit for. So your dad might not have been proud, but I am. You've succeeded in ways that he couldn't. They go far beyond renovating an abandoned mill. You're a fine man, Josh. A good father and, from what I hear, a fair businessman and a loyal friend. Your dad was none of those. You are a good man."

"Thank you," Josh said and cleared his throat when emotion threatened to take over. "I appreciate hearing that." He did, more than he could say.

It wasn't as if he didn't realize that growing up with an abusive father had affected him. Sometimes he was still surprised at the depth to which his father's aggression and his ex-wife's rejection colored his view of himself and his worth.

"I hope things go well with that California company." Rudy's eyes were knowing. "I'm not always a fan of change, but you deserve whatever opportunity comes your way."

Josh thanked the man again, then entered his brother's firm with a new sense of purpose. No matter what he decided about this opportunity or his future in general, he had a better understanding that he did deserve the good things that might come his way. In business and life and most certainly in love.

Chapter Fifteen

Two days later, Ella pulled up to her father's house as the first pinks of the approaching dawn colored the sky.

He didn't know about her plan for the day because she hadn't been sure she'd have the courage to go through with it. Now that she was here, she couldn't deny that it felt right—or at least it would if her father agreed. She got out of the car. As she approached the house, the door opened. Jack stood at the threshold.

"This is a surprise," he said, one thick brow raising. He wore trim khaki pants and a navy blue polo, his summer uniform for as many years as she could remember. When she was younger, she thought he was prematurely stodgy. Today it felt like a comfort of sorts.

"I heard you were heading to Seattle for some tests."

He shrugged like it was no big deal. "Seems like a good day for a drive into the city."

She nodded. "That's what I thought as well. I was hoping you'd be up for company?"

His jaw dropped open for a moment before he quickly snapped it shut. "I'd like that."

"We'll take your car," she said. "But I'll drive."

Her small hatchback was efficient but nowhere near as comfortable or responsive as his sleek Mercedes sedan.

"Do you have a problem with my driving, young lady?" he asked, stepping back to allow her into the house.

"You drove like an old man even before you were one," she told him.

He chuckled. "Have you ever heard of the saying you catch more flies with honey than vinegar?"

She shrugged. "Yeah, but I'm not looking to catch flies."

"Duly noted. Are you interested in a cup of coffee for the road?"

"Sure."

He poured her a generous serving into a to-go thermos.

Ella grabbed a granola bar from the pantry. "I hope you don't mind."

"This is still your house," her father said, his voice as gentle as she'd ever heard it. "You are welcome to anything I have."

A strange sort of emotion welled in her at his words, but she swallowed it down with the first swig of coffee.

As they took off on the highway that led over the pass and toward the city, Ella breathed out a sigh. She'd been worried that her dad was going to want to overanalyze the meaning behind her offer to accompany him to Seattle. For the moment, he seemed content to watch morning break over the valley as it spread out before them.

"I've seen some pretty fantastic sunrises in the past couple of years," she said, breaking the silence. "Nothing compares to the light around Starlight."

"I think Dorothy Gale had it right after all," her father answered. "There's no place like home."

"As long as there are no flying monkeys involved," she agreed, and they both laughed. Before her mother died, one of the few family activities Jack had made time for was the movie nights her mom liked to schedule.

He would often be working on his computer, and at the time, young Ella had wondered why he'd even bothered showing up. She recently understood that in his own way, he'd been making an effort and that was what counted.

She wished she'd appreciated the fact earlier.

"Not to look a gift passenger in the mouth," Jack

said as she continued driving, "but did your brother put you up to this?"

Old Ella would have been offended by the suggestion and the fact that he'd made it, even if it was true. She shrugged. "He doesn't know I'm here. If he did, he'd probably think I offered to come with you so I could let you off on the side of the road someplace to fend for yourself the way you did with us after Mom died."

She bit down on her lower lip and immediately regretted her words. Her father had been nothing but kind this morning when he had every right to turn her away. She'd promised herself that she would be civil today. This was about aiding her dad or at least making a little peace with him.

Her comment wasn't peaceful in any manner.

"I'm sorry," they said at the same time.

She sighed. "It's the past. I should leave it there. You've apologized, Dad. This is my problem now."

"Your problem is my problem."

"I still can't get used to you being a good person," she admitted. "It might help if you could be a jerk for a few minutes. Give me a dismissive or judgmental comment so I can feel balanced again. More like myself."

"You are more yourself when I'm the enemy?" Her father shook his head. "Did I mess things up so badly for you, Ella?"

She swallowed back the emotion clogging her throat. "It wasn't you, Dad. You weren't exactly a candidate for father of the year, but the accident is what started it all for me. You were an easy target for my anger over losing Mom."

"Because I couldn't get past my grief to help you through yours." Jack reached out a hand to touch the window when a leaf blew against it. "It was more than me not being fit for a parenting award. My most important task after your mom died was to take care of you and your brother. To support you. I thought giving you material things was enough."

"I didn't exactly make it easy on you." Ella felt like it was necessary to own up to her part in what was wrong between them.

"No." Jack shook his head. "You were a child. You had no responsibility in this."

Her heart appreciated hearing the words, but they also made her feel ashamed for wasting so much time in anger. Her resentment hadn't gotten her anywhere, and she was no longer a child. Her father still looked robust and healthy despite his brush with cancer, but he wasn't ageless. His hair was almost entirely gray now, and deep lines fanned out from the corners of his eyes.

He remained an attractive man but no longer seemed immortal the way he had when Ella was a girl. If Ella was going to make things right between them, now was the time. She couldn't wait.

"Mom would have been disappointed in me," she said softly. "That's maybe the worst part. Even as

I was acting out, I knew my behavior would have brought her pain."

"She would have found a way to make it better," her father answered. "Because that's what she did for all of us."

Ella sniffed. "All I wanted to do was make it better or at least numb myself against how badly it hurt. Except everything I tried was stupid and reckless."

"Until nursing," her father supplied.

They'd come to the main interstate now, and she concentrated on the passing cars and the road in front of them.

"I wanted to help make people better," she agreed with a nod. "Even that didn't work out the way I planned. There were kids I couldn't help. Patients we couldn't save."

"I'm sure there were many more you did save. Who you did help. People probably think of you as an angel who came into their life."

Ella gave her father an arch look, and he laughed. "Okay, angel might be a stretch. You know what I mean, El."

"I had a baby named after me once," she told him. "A boy we treated for a nearly fatal snakebite. His mom was pregnant, and a week after the big brother was seen at the clinic, she went into labor. I helped deliver the baby…"

"And she named her Ella?" Jack beamed.

Ella laughed and shook her head. "Actually, she named the baby Sam. It was a boy. But the mother told me it was because of my last name being Samuelson."

"That's amazing. Your mother would have been proud of what you've done." Her father cleared his throat. "I'm proud, Ella. Not that it means anything to you, but I want you to know. If you take nothing else when you leave, at least carry that with you."

"It means something. I'm still angry, Dad. I've carried this bitterness around for a long time, and I think it's going to take some work for me to let it go. I want to try, though."

"I'm not perfect," her dad answered. "I'm sure I'll continue to bumble along, but as long as we both try, it will be better than the alternative. No matter how far away in the world you're called, you'll always have a home in Starlight. And no matter how long you stay away, Finn and I will always be your family. Kaitlyn now, too. You aren't alone. I know it felt like that after Mom died. At least it felt like that for me. But neither of us is alone."

Ella nodded and tightened her grip on the steering wheel. She wanted to trust her dad's promise. Maybe this was the new start she needed to do just that.

Still, it felt as though every time she allowed herself to believe she wasn't alone, the person she had come to depend on left her. Whether it was her mother or a man. Even Josh with his new, perfect potential girlfriend. He owed her nothing, and she understood that they couldn't be together in any real way, but her heart still felt betrayed that he could even consider another relationship.

Trusting her father's words wouldn't come easy, but it was essential to heal, not only for the sake of their relationship but to fix all the ways she'd let herself put up defenses.

"You think that clam chowder place Mom used to work at across from the Pike Place Market is still there?" she asked as the first view of the city appeared as she crested a rise on the interstate.

One of the other things her mother had insisted on was going back-to-school shopping each year in Seattle. Ella had loved the day spent with her mom in the city, and they'd always had lunch at the same downtown restaurant. It was the place where her parents had met when Katie had been waitressing there during college. Katie and Jack had gone on their first date during one of her mother's breaks.

Jack nodded. "Their bread bowls are just as great as they were back in the day."

"Well, then after we get your clean bill of health, we're going to go clog our arteries and carb overload with some soup in a bread bowl."

He laughed again. "It's a deal."

Ella felt her grasp on the steering wheel loosen, along with something that felt like it had been lodged deep in her chest since her mother's accident.

She might not have all the answers she wanted, but this day with her dad was the start of something new. She would be able to leave Starlight knowing she could always come home.

Somehow she expected the thought would make her trepidation about leaving ease, but instead it seemed to heighten it. The happier she felt in her life, the harder it was to think of walking away.

By the time Josh and Anna arrived at Tall Pines Camp on Saturday night for Tessa and Carson's engagement party, the festivities were already in full swing.

"See how late we are, Daddy," his daughter complained. "All the boats are already out on the lake."

"People will bring in the canoes, Banana. You'll get your turn."

"We're so late. I told Evie I would be here right away. What if she doesn't have anybody to talk to?"

Josh could see Evie and Tyler, Brynn Dunlap's son of the same age, playing badminton in the meadow next to the picnic tables. "Evie is fine, sweetheart."

"What if she and Tyler don't want me to play with them now?"

Josh blinked. He'd never heard so much as a peep of self-doubt from his confident daughter. So much so that he hadn't considered Anna could feel unsure of herself in any situation. He unbuckled the seat belt and turned to face her in the back of the truck. Anna stared out the window, her mouth set in a mulish frown.

"Evie is your best friend. She will always make

room for you in whatever she's doing. Just like you would do for her. What's going on, Anna-banana? Did you and Evie get in a fight?"

Anna shook her head. "But stupid Aubrey and her friends sat down with Evie at lunch yesterday. When I got there, they told me there wasn't any room at the table."

Josh's heart plummeted in his chest. He hadn't heard anything about those girls since the sleepover party that Anna had chosen to leave. He'd stupidly assumed that meant there would be no repercussions for his daughter.

His dad had been the ultimate bully, so Josh should have known there were always consequences, even if a person couldn't see them immediately. For all of Anna's confidence, she was a sweet soul who'd been through more than any child should have to withstand. He hated the thought of her being upset about anything, let alone petty schoolgirl drama.

"What did Evie do?" he asked cautiously.

Anna's thin arms wrapped around her stomach. "She scooted over to make room for me, but I told her I didn't wanna sit with them. Then I didn't have anybody to sit with because everybody was already sitting with people so I went to the bathroom and ate my lunch by myself and it was awful and then I didn't want to go out to recess because I knew Evie would say something and Aubrey and her friends would be watching and now I've messed everything up."

His daughter had spoken so fast he'd barely kept

up. The issue didn't seem to be a huge one, but it obviously meant a lot to Anna. Not for the first time, he cursed his ex-wife for walking away from their daughter and showing very little interest in Anna's life since the divorce.

He could deal with Jenn leaving him. He could even forgive her for having a breakdown when Anna had battled cancer. It wasn't right, although he understood people dealt with trauma in different ways. But Anna needed a mom who cared on a consistent basis, not just when her schedule allowed.

Jenn was a fan of popping into their lives and then taking off again whenever the mood suited her. He hadn't been oblivious to how it might be affecting Anna as she got older but figured he could make up for any deficiency on her mother's part.

Emotions and self-esteem didn't work that way. Of all people, he should know that. His mom had cared for him and Parker, but it hadn't changed who his father was or how his abuse and neglect had shaped Josh.

If anything, this moment made him consider the thought of a stable relationship in his life even more seriously. He wanted a woman who would make Anna, as well as him, a priority.

It wasn't as if he could rely on Mara forever. She had her own daughter, and she and his brother were interested in adding to their family, potentially through adoption. Mara would never purposely make

Anna feel like less of a priority, but how could that be avoided?

Maybe using Anna as his primary motivation wasn't exactly showing the best intentions as he put himself out in the dating world again. It wasn't as if he only wanted a woman to take care of his daughter. Frankly, he didn't trust himself to choose a woman who would be kind to his kid.

Jenn had been a fine mom before she'd decided she wasn't going to anymore. She'd never been the cookie-baking, kiss-your-boo-boos-better type, but they'd muddled along fine. What did it say about his standards that muddling along felt like the best he could expect?

A flash of red caught his eye, and he sucked in a breath as he realized it was Ella in a modest two-piece swimsuit covered by short denim cutoffs. She was laughing at something Rob said, and her effortless beauty made Josh almost light-headed, like he was spinning on an amusement park ride.

She would know what to tell Anna about standing up to the mean girls, but how could he ask her to intervene when he was trying to put more distance between them? Space he didn't want, but that seemed necessary anyway.

He offered his daughter a gentle smile. "If you want to go home, say the word. I can explain that something came up with work."

It was a ridiculous offer. What kind of dad was he to encourage his kid to lie and run from her problems?

"It's your stupid job that made us late in the first place."

"Anna, enough with the word *stupid*."

She blinked. "Okay, I'm going to go talk to Evie."

She climbed out of the car without another word, leaving him wondering where he'd lost control of that conversation. It felt as though they'd gone from a borderline crisis of confidence to pulling up the proverbial bootstraps with one stern comment on his part.

Maybe that was good. He was being a consistent parent, sending a message that they could talk about feelings but not disparage other people in the process.

Or maybe Anna had banked this moment somewhere in her unconscious for a later day. She would pull out the hardships of her childhood to examine them like a marble collection. Cancer. Mom leaving. Dad a complete emotional moron.

Add it to her list.

He approached the activity centered on the picnic area with caution. These were his friends, and he knew he had a home here, but for the first time in his life, Josh wondered if Starlight was indeed the place where he belonged.

He'd never doubted it before but felt like he was receiving repeated signs that the time might be right to try something new. That forcing himself to live up to other people's expectations made life more challenging than it was supposed to be.

His mother would have warned that he was reading more into the moment, trying to take responsibility for things that weren't his fault. She'd tell him that Anna's social troubles couldn't be linked to any deficiencies in Josh's parenting. He wasn't sure anymore.

"How did things go with the California company?" Finn Samuelson asked as he handed Josh a beer. "They're a major player in the commercial real estate space in this region. The fact that a couple of the higher-ups made the trip to Starlight to talk to you says a lot about how serious they are regarding this deal."

Josh took a small sip and thought about how to answer. This would likely be his only drink for the day, so he wanted to savor it. "It went fine. They had stipulations and I had stipulations, but we're still moving forward. I'm not convinced it's the right move, but I'm open to the possibility."

"You should be proud of yourself," his brother's best friend said easily. "It's a big vote of confidence in what you built here to have a firm of that size interested in partnering with you."

"More like acquiring me." Josh lifted the beer can to his mouth, then lowered it again. "That's the problem. I like what I've built. I like the jobs we're doing and the control I have over things. I have a great crew and strong relationships with the best subcontractors in the area. Part of my company's success is me, and if I give it over to some out-of-state corporation, that changes everything."

Finn chose a pretzel from one of the bowls of

snacks on the picnic table. "Change isn't always a bad thing."

"Maybe," Josh acknowledged. He looked for Anna and found her tugging a canoe toward the water along with Evie and Tyler. His daughter was smiling and laughing. All of her earlier worries apparently melted away.

He wished it were that easy for himself.

"It's different for you," he told Finn, turning to face the man more fully. "You left Starlight just like Parker did, so when you came back everyone was excited to have you here. They don't feel like you owe them anything. I'm guessing you don't feel like you owe them anything."

"Owe who?" Finn asked, looking genuinely confused.

"The town."

"You owe the entire town? For what?"

"People around here have taken care of me my whole life in one way or another. Even if I don't literally leave, selling out to a big company feels like selling out on my community."

Finn shook his head. "Since when is it your responsibility to take care of the whole community?"

Josh took a long breath then told Finn what he hadn't even discussed with his own brother. "A couple of the current council members approached me about running for mayor. Curtis wants to retire so won't be seeking reelection for another term."

"Do you want to be mayor?"

"Do you think I can't handle it? My father certainly would have hated the idea."

"I think you would be great if it's what you want. I think it would be unfortunate if your dad is the reason you say yes."

Josh laughed at that. "Like I said, my dad would not support me running for mayor."

"That's my point," Finn said. "Would you say yes because it's an opportunity you want or would you say yes to prove something to your dead father?"

When Josh frowned, Finn held up his hands. "I'm not making a judgment, simply asking the question. I'm the local banker's son. I spent most of my adult life as a bitter workaholic doing a job I didn't care about so I could prove I was better than my old man. Not everyone knows why the Dennison Mill meant so much to you, Josh, but I do. Parker and I were friends at the time the company pulled out, and your father's reaction to it is burned in my brain. He made my dad look like some sort of sitcom father. It wasn't pretty, and that was the sliver I saw from the outside."

"It wasn't pretty at all. Why shouldn't I take an opportunity to prove that I'm nothing like him but could do the same job he did with even more success?"

"That doesn't answer the question of whether it's a job you want."

"At this very moment, I want to walk away from all of it. I want to make a condition of this deal with the California company that I move to a new location. Start over with Anna and me in a place where no one knows our history. We can be the people we are today. A dad who has his life together with his adorable, healthy daughter."

"Do you think it would be so easy to leave it all behind?"

"No." Josh sighed. "Right now, nothing feels easy, and that's the worst part."

"Then fix it," Finn told him. "No one can do that for you. Nobody else knows what's going to make it better. But the situation will only improve if you make it so."

As if on cue, he looked toward the dock and saw Ella standing there. She glanced at Josh like she could feel his gaze on her. Her smile, even though it was slight, warmed him to his toes. He thought about making things better, and his heart insisted she would have something to do with that.

Chapter Sixteen

Ella glanced behind her as a familiar truck pulled to a stop behind her car on the shoulder of the mountain pass. It was nearly nine at night, and shadows were quickly expanding their reach, making visibility worse with every passing second.

"Here, doggy," she called into the thick woods that lined either side of the road. "Come out so you don't get run over."

There was no response other than the sound of the wind through the trees. She turned as Josh and Anna approached.

"Car trouble?" Josh asked, concern lacing his tone.

Two simple words and she was practically ready to melt in a puddle at his feet. Truly pathetic, but

Ella felt raw and exposed at this moment, and not just because of the location.

There weren't many vehicles on this part of the mountain at night. She'd stayed behind after the end of the party at Tall Pines to help clean up and discuss a few more details for Tessa's wedding next week.

"My car is fine," she answered. "What are you two doing up here?"

Anna's skinny shoulders rose and fell. "I left Hippo at camp today, so we're going back to get him."

Ella hid her smile. In the couple of times she'd been with Anna during her bedtime routine, she knew the girl had given the name Hippo to her favorite stuffed elephant.

"Hippo is lucky to have you to look out for him."

Anna nodded. "He wanted to watch everyone at the picnic, so I got him out of the truck. The last thing I told him when I put him on a boulder was, 'Stay right there. I'll be back.' We have to go get him."

Josh's crooked smile made Ella's insides tumble even more. "No stuffed animal left behind," he said.

"Or stray animal," Ella murmured, looking at the woods again. Had she just seen movement behind that far tree?

"Come again?" Josh and Anna followed her gaze, but it was clear neither of them saw anything.

"I was driving home, and I swear I saw a dog race

across the road and into the trees. I pulled over to try to find him or her."

"Are you sure it wasn't a raccoon or fox?" Josh asked. "There are a lot of animals around here."

Ella shook her head. "I'm positive it was a dog, and I'm guessing someone dumped it. Wouldn't be the first time."

"Why would the dog's owner do that?" Anna asked the question as if she couldn't fathom it.

"Some people are jerks," Ella said. "But the dog could be injured or hungry. And if it darts out into the road and a driver swerves, well…"

She tried to make it sound like she was giving the facts but had a feeling Josh understood what that scenario meant to her. Her mom had been killed in a car crash driving Finn to football practice. She'd swerved, trying to avoid hitting a deer, and then lost control of the car.

"We need to find it." Anna took her father's hand and tugged. "I left my lunch box in the back seat. I bet if the dog's hungry, he'll want the old crusts I didn't eat."

"You're supposed to eat the crusts," Josh told his daughter. "But in this case, it's a good thing you didn't."

Emotion welled in Ella. "You two don't need to stay. I'll find—"

"We're staying," Josh said without hesitation. "Let's not waste the remaining daylight by arguing."

She nodded. "Thank you."

"Banana, stay close to Ella while I'm at the truck. This road isn't busy, but it's still not my favorite thing to have you walking along the side of it."

"We'll head into the trees." Ella reached for the girl's hand, not giving the gesture a second thought.

Anna transferred her grip from her dad to Ella.

As Josh jogged back to the truck, she led the girl a few steps onto a narrow game path that disappeared into the forest.

"Here, doggy," she called and then whistled.

"You're not a good whistler," Anna advised her. "Keep calling to it."

Ella didn't take offense to the girl's bluntness. She actually liked it.

They walked forward a few more paces, and Anna froze. "I saw something," she whispered, pointing to a clump of bushes with several fallen logs lying in front of them.

Ella stilled, and they both listened. After a moment, there was an almost indiscernible sound of leaves crunching. Anna squeezed her hand.

"Got the crusts," Josh announced.

Ella and Anna turned as one to hush him.

He handed Ella the plastic bag of day-old bread when she gestured for it. She tore off a piece and tossed it in the direction of the fallen logs.

Josh came to stand behind her, the heat from his body offering a strange sort of comfort in the moment.

She was almost—but not quite—positive about what she'd seen on the road. In reality, she could be chasing after a wild animal that was just fine without her interference.

A minute stretched as the three of them watched the spot where Anna had seen movement. Ella stifled a gasp when a medium-sized mutt of indiscriminate breed eased out from behind the bushes. The dog glanced at them and then quickly away. None of them moved as the animal cautiously approached the food.

He or she sniffed it and then gobbled it up, tail wagging.

"Good boy," Anna crooned as the dog swallowed. "Or girl. You're a sweet doggy. Would you come over here so we can look at you? We're really nice. At least Daddy's really nice. Ella and I are kinda nice when we want to be."

Ella felt rather than heard Josh's quiet laugh against the back of her neck.

"She's not wrong," he whispered.

"Focus," Ella retorted, and her heart leaped inside her chest as the animal lifted its head to scent the air, then trotted forward.

"You're a dog whisperer," she told Anna, and the girl encouraged the dog to keep moving toward them.

"Don't get too close," Josh warned. "We don't know anything about the animal yet."

The dog seemed to hear the warning and slowed its progression. Then, just before reaching them, the animal flipped on its back and offered up a too-skinny belly.

"Well, he's a boy," Josh said with a chuckle.

Anna started to move forward, but Ella placed a hand on her shoulder. "Let me go first," she told the girl.

"Or me," Josh suggested, but Ella was already bending down.

"It's okay, honey." She glanced up at Josh. "Sometimes dogs react more to men." The only reaction the dog seemed ready to offer was intense joy. He wiggled on his back and then turned to one side, gently licking Ella's hand as she stroked along his side.

"He doesn't have a collar," she noted, "but maybe he's been chipped. I'm not supposed to have animals at my rental, but I can bring him to my dad's for the night and call the vet in the morning."

"He can come home with us," Anna offered. When she crouched down next to Ella, the dog nuzzled against her.

"He's dirty and stinky," Ella told the girl. "You might not want to deal with that."

"I don't care about dirty and stinky," Anna said firmly. "I'll give him a bath. What do you think we should name him?"

"We're not naming him anything," Josh said to his daughter. "This is not our dog."

"But what if he doesn't have anybody?" Anna insisted. "He just wants somebody to love on him."

Although Ella had nothing in common with a stray mutt, somehow she could relate.

The sound of a horn from the road startled all of

them. The dog hopped to his feet, and Ella worried he might take off again.

He trembled but didn't move. She reached out to him. "You're a sweet boy. You must have belonged to somebody at some point." She looked at Anna. "He's too friendly to have been on his own for long."

"Come on, boy," she said, patting her leg as she straightened and hoping the dog would follow.

"I brought rope from the back of the truck if you want to make a leash," Josh offered.

"Let's see if he'll come on his own," Ella answered. "I don't want to freak him out any more than he probably already is."

As she'd hoped, the dog seemed happy to follow them back toward the road.

"Please, Daddy." Anna used her sweetest pleading tone. "Can he please stay the night at our house?"

Ella had no doubt that Josh was going to give in, and a moment later he nodded. "Only for the night, and he sleeps in the laundry room. What are we going to do about picking up Hippo? I don't think it's a good idea to have this dog driving all over the mountain."

"Ella and I will take him back to our house," Anna said as if it were already a done deal. "You can get Hippo and then come down."

Ella stifled a laugh. The girl certainly had moxie.

Josh met her gaze over Anna's head. "Is that okay with you?"

"Sure. Why don't you take a couple of photos of

him on your phone in case Kayla and Rob recognize him?" After Josh snapped the pics, she unlatched the hatch on her car and the dog hopped up.

They transferred Anna's booster seat to Ella's car, and the girl climbed in. Before the back door was even shut, the dog had hopped over the seat and did its best to climb into Anna's lap. The kid didn't care one bit about the animal being dirty. She stroked his matted head with her small hand.

"Here we are on another adventure." Josh smiled as his daughter's laugh sounded from inside the car.

Ella couldn't quite read his tone. "Sorry to drag you in. I'm sure you have way better things to do tonight than deal with a stray."

She started around her car, but Josh's hand on her arm stopped her.

"I don't have anything better to do," he said gently, and once more she cursed her reaction to him.

Friends, she reminded herself. That's all they were. She nodded and climbed in the car, then started down the mountain.

"You need to work on your willpower before she gets to high school," Ella announced as Josh entered the family room after tucking Anna into bed. "She's going to have her teenage way with her pushover daddy otherwise."

He rolled his eyes and chuckled. "Maybe, but I'm not keeping that dog."

Ella was sitting on his sofa with her legs crisscrossed in front of her. All three of them had gotten soaking wet when they bathed the dog. Ella wore one of his old T-shirts and a pair of his sweatpants. His body had the strangest reaction to seeing her in his clothes. The chant of "mine" had pounded across his brain like a drum for the past hour as they'd worked on settling both the animal and Anna.

He had meant to stick with the plan of leaving the dog in the mudroom overnight, but he'd whined and scratched at the door when they put him away.

"Maybe he needs to go out," Ella had suggested. As soon as Josh cracked open the door, the animal had found his way through and scampered up the stairs. By the time Josh caught up with him, the dog was curled in a neat ball at the end of Anna's bed. Yes, Josh was a pushover. He couldn't help it.

"I'll come by in the morning and pick him up," Ella said as she started to stand.

Josh held out a hand. "Don't go yet." He thought she might ignore his request but then she settled back against the couch cushions. "Can I get you a drink after all that adventure?"

She shook her head. "I'm fine."

There it was again—that thread of uncertainty in her voice.

It was like hearing Anna doubt herself—completely foreign to what he thought of as Ella's true personality. He didn't care for it and liked even less the thought that he'd caused it.

"What are the chances that dog has a home with people who want him back?" he asked.

"He should. To me, he looks a little underweight, but he's been well cared for until recently. Hopefully, the vet will be able to tell us more in the morning. I appreciate you keeping him here."

"Would you have really taken him to your dad's?"

Her features gentled at the mention of her father, which surprised Josh.

"Yeah. My dad and I are doing a little better."

"When did that happen?"

"I drove him to Seattle to have his regular testing. We had a good talk on the way. I'm not saying things are perfect but a little better. And even more importantly, all of his tests were good."

"I'm glad on both counts." Josh wasn't lying, but his reaction felt more complicated than those simple words. Of course he was happy if she was working things out with her father, but he hated that he hadn't known about it. That something monumental had happened in Ella's life, and he hadn't been privy to it, not that he had any right.

"So things are going well with Crystal?" she asked.

He did not want to talk about Crystal with Ella but felt like he had to answer the question. "We're taking it slow."

"But it's going well," she insisted like she was trying to prove something to them both.

He nodded. "How are your plans for going back to

work? Not too much longer now." He felt the need to remind her that she was the one leaving. She was the one who didn't want a relationship with him, and he was through trying to give his heart to people who didn't want it.

She glanced away. "Fine."

"Why do I feel like that word holds a hidden meaning?"

Her mouth curved at the corners. "Oh, you think you know me so well." Her smile faded. "Maybe you do. They sent me the new contract, but I haven't signed it yet."

His heart seemed to skip a beat as she spoke the words. "What does that mean?"

"Probably nothing." She stretched her arms above her head, revealing the tiniest sliver of her stomach where his shirt rode up. "It probably means that I'm trash at committing to something and still letting fear rule my life."

"Could it mean that you don't want to leave Starlight?" He moved closer to her and half expected her to shy away.

Instead, when he cupped his hands on either side of her face, she leaned in. Now it wasn't just his heart stammering. His whole body seemed to be on high alert.

"I'm tired of letting fear control my life," she whispered, nearly touching her mouth to his.

"Then let it go, sweetheart. Just let go."

As much as Josh wanted to kiss her, he didn't.

This would have to be her choice. He wasn't going to try to force her to want him the way he wanted her.

But when her lips pressed against his, he couldn't help his groan of pleasure. Nothing compared to Ella and how she made him want to open his heart again and forget his fear. To be brave for her. To be better for her.

The kiss deepened as their tongues melded. In spite of the need pounding through him, he was content to savor and sip. He knew enough about them both to understand coming together didn't equate to any guarantees. That was the risk when flying. Would the wind carry him, or was he sailing on wax wings that would leave him plummeting to earth when he got too close to the sun?

Ella was his light. And as their breathing intensified, he could feel desire pulsing through her the same way it poured through his veins.

Without a word, he stood and offered his hand. He didn't hide anything from his gaze and knew she would understand what it meant to take his hand.

To his great relief, she slipped her fingers into his. He led her up the stairs and into his bedroom, then left her for a moment to check on Anna, which possibly made him a fool. He was wasting precious minutes on parenting duties, but this was his life.

Anna being a priority didn't make him less of a man. There would never be a time with any woman when he forgot about his daughter or his duty. The dog lifted his head as Josh opened the door but didn't move. Anna's fingers were wrapped around her stuffed animal, and the stray seemed perfectly content with his place on the bed watching over them both.

Josh wasn't sure whether to hope they found the animal's family or not. Would it be so awful to add a pet to their little family? Whether they stayed in Starlight or tried a new life in California with the partnership, a pet could move with them, right?

Any questions about the future faded when he returned to the bedroom. Ella was already in his bed, her bare shoulders peeking out from the sheet she'd drawn up over her.

God, he liked having her there.

He stripped down, pulled a condom from the nightstand drawer then joined her in bed after unrolling it down his length.

"I can't stay the night," she said as he drew her closer. "It wouldn't be right for Anna to wake up with me here."

"My focus is right now," he said, kissing her jaw then trailing kisses along her throat to the lovely ridge of her collarbone.

"Now is good," she whispered, her voice husky. "I've got at least five minutes to spare."

He glanced up at her, and his heart skipped a beat at the teasing grin she wore. "Why does that sound like a challenge?"

Her smile widened. "Are you…um…up for it?"

He laughed. Leave it to Ella to turn sex into something even better than a simple act of joining—which was pretty good in and of itself. But the fact that they could laugh and joke made it even more special. "I guess you'll have to wait and see." He shifted the sheet until her breasts were revealed and kissed one puckered tip. She let out a moan, which turned into a tiny sound of distress when he paused.

"For the record, you're going to have to wait a lot longer than five minutes, Ella."

She smoothed away a lock of hair that had fallen in his face. "As long as you make the wait worth it," she told him, less teasing and more commanding warrior goddess. He liked her even more this way.

"Oh, I intend to," he said, then returned his attention to doing just that.

Chapter Seventeen

"Ella, can I talk to you for a minute?"

Ella glanced up from the paperwork she was completing on Monday morning and motioned Kayla into the nurse's office. "Of course. If this is about the cabins that still need cleaning, I'm going to get to them right after lunch. I got a late start today because of Grover."

The Tall Pines owner smiled. "I'm glad the vet was able to help you reunite him with his family."

"Me, too." She tried to muster a smidge more joy that the dog had gone home. Grover, as she'd discovered was his name, belonged to a young couple with three kids under the age of ten who lived in the next town over. According to the sweet and somewhat scattered woman who'd come to pick him up, one of her kids had left the back gate open when they'd been visiting her mother in Starlight. The dog had run off, and they'd been looking for him for the better part of a week.

Ella hadn't wanted to sound judgmental when the woman seemed to be both grateful to have their beloved dog returning and flustered in the way of moms of young kids. Still, she couldn't resist asking why there hadn't been more signs up or notifications of a lost dog on the pet websites.

The woman had apologized and sounded like she was about to cry when she'd explained that her middle son had just been diagnosed with autism, and she was up to her eyeballs trying to make a plan with the school.

Ella had then felt like a completely insensitive jerk. In truth, she was thinking about Anna's reaction to losing the dog. But the animal was ecstatic to be reunited with his human mom, so Ella knew she'd done the right thing in taking him to the vet to be scanned for a chip.

Anna was somewhere on the camp property since she and Evie were doing another session.

Ella had texted Josh to tell him the outcome. A day had passed, but she wasn't sure how well Anna had dealt with the news. Hiding out in the nurse's office seemed easier than facing the disappointment or recrimination in the girl's eyes since Ella had been the one to help find Grover's family. *Wimp*, she mentally scolded herself, then turned her attention back to Kayla.

"What can I do for you?"

"I'll warn you in advance," the woman said with an almost nervous laugh, "it's a big ask."

She stepped into the room, followed by a handsome man who looked to be in his midthirties. "Ella, I'd like you to meet Dr. Eric Steadman. He recently transferred to Starlight Valley Hospital from Houston."

"That's a significant change," Ella murmured, standing up to shake hands with the doctor.

He had close-cropped blond hair and piercing green eyes. She had no doubt he was a doctor in real life, but the man also would have been a welcome addition to any ridiculously good-looking ensemble television cast.

"I wanted to get out of the city," Eric told her. "And Starlight seemed like the perfect place for a new start."

"You aren't wrong." Ella gave Kayla a questioning look. "What can I do for the two of you?"

"I'm heading up a new pediatric oncology division locally, but I'm also working with one of the larger medical campuses out of Seattle on a few outreach projects."

"Mmm-hmm." An uncomfortable sense of foreboding crept along Ella's spine. She wasn't sure where this conversation was going but got the distinct impression she wouldn't like the outcome.

"They want to offer a weekend camp for kids with cancer here at Tall Pines," Kayla explained as if she could discern Ella's growing discomfort with the conversation.

Eric nodded. "We'd invite some of the patients, as well as their families, to camp for a couple of days. All expenses paid by the hospital's foundation. It would be a trial run, and if things go well, we're interested in expanding the program for next summer."

"It would be a break from what they're going through." Kayla gave Ella a hopeful smile. "Rob and I would love to help out in this way."

"Sometimes weeks or months of treatment is almost as hard on a child's caregiver as on the actual patient." Eric's face was the picture of compassion. "The sense of responsibility and worry, plus the inherent difficulty of watching a son or daughter suffer, can be a burden on the parents and other siblings."

Ella thought about what she'd experienced with the parents of dying children and swallowed down the emotion threatening to clog her throat. "I don't know what this has to do with me."

"We're targeting the weekend after Tessa's wedding, just before you're scheduled to leave town," Kayla said. "I'm hoping you'll say yes to helping run the weekend."

Ella automatically shook her head. "I can't."

Eric took a step closer. "Kayla has told me about some of your experience with nursing. Seattle General will be sending staff to look after patients while they're here, and most of the kids attending will be either finished with treatment or at least medically cleared to take part. But it would be a huge advantage to have someone on-site with a medical background who also knows the camp and the area."

"There are plenty of nurses at the local hospital." She gave Eric an obvious once-over. "I'm sure most of them would say yes to anything you ask."

The insinuation of the comment was rude, and by the way his eyes narrowed, Ella could tell she'd shocked him. She didn't care. She wanted to shock or offend this stranger, anything to get him to leave her alone.

"I was the one who suggested we ask you." The admonishment in Kayla's voice was unmistakable. "It would mean a lot to Rob and me if you'd help, Ella."

If Ella's barometer for how to live her life was the question "What would Katie Samuelson do," there was no question as to the answer. Her mother would want and expect that Ella step up and step in to help Kayla in whatever way she needed.

That's how Katie had lived her life, always willing to give and contribute to the Starlight community.

But Ella wasn't her mother, and she only had a few short weeks before she left this town in her rearview mirror for good.

Still, she couldn't help but nod. It was the right thing to do and what her mother would want. "Okay. But if the program continues next summer, you'll have to find someone else." She gave the good doctor a pointed look. "I'm leaving."

"Understood," he said. "All we need is a successful start to this program, and I think you'll be a huge part of that. We're having a meeting at the hospital tomorrow afternoon to discuss the details and formulate an action plan for the weekend. There isn't a lot of time to make sure everything comes together."

"It will more than come together," Kayla promised him. "With Ella's help, the weekend is sure to be a huge success."

The man let out a noticeable sigh of relief. "Thank you both. I'll see you tomorrow."

Ella crossed her arms over her chest, thrust out her hip and glared at Kayla after Dr. Steadman disappeared down the hall. "I'm leaving," she said, her tone flat. "You can come up with a dozen other projects for me to work on before I go, but that won't change the reality. I'm not staying in Starlight, Kayla."

"This is your home," the older woman said. "Your dad told me the two of you worked out some things. Doesn't that make a difference? Your mother—"

"Is dead," Ella supplied. "I'm not looking to follow in her footsteps and devote myself to this town. I wasn't meant to stay."

Kayla's pink-glossed lips pressed together. "It worries me to no end to think of you gallivanting all over the globe. It's not safe, Ella. What kind of friend would I be to your mother if I didn't try to keep you safe?"

Tears stung the back of Ella's eyes. She knew Kayla meant well and appreciated the woman's concern. Maybe Ella wouldn't have made the life choices—or some of the mistakes—she had if her mom was still alive. If that loss hadn't shaped the person she was and limited what she was able to give.

But her mom wasn't here, and no one could change the past. "There are no guarantees," she said quietly. "The car accident that killed my mother is a perfect example. I wish I could be the person everyone wants and expects me to be. I wish I could be more like her." She drew in a breath when her voice cracked. "I'm not her."

"I know," Kayla agreed, squeezing Ella's shoulder. "I don't want you to be someone you aren't, dear. I do expect you to try to be happy, and you have yet to convince me that heading off into the wild blue yonder is going to accomplish that."

Ella wasn't so sure either, but she'd committed to going even if she hadn't yet signed the contract. The alternative—staying—would mean more than she was willing to risk.

Ella sat on the soft ground in front of her mother's statue later that week and stared up at the sky above her, which was streaked with ribbons of orange and purple as the sun began to set.

She'd witnessed a thousand sunsets in a dozen different countries during her time as a traveling nurse, but the vibrant colors that infused the sky around her hometown remained her favorite. Golden hour, she'd heard this time of day called, and tonight that moniker fit.

Memories of her childhood played on an endless reel in her mind, hued with their own sort of golden hour light, soft and serene.

Since when had making her mom proud become such a North Star in her life? In the years after the accident, anger and grief had propelled Ella to do everything she could to distance herself from the person her mother would have wanted or expected her to be.

She'd shrugged off the mantle a long time ago, or so she'd thought.

This summer had suddenly shown her that rejecting the constraints of other people's desires for her was just another form of running. She ran away instead of trying or putting her heart at risk because of what it might mean. The rejection or failure that could result.

On the surface, no one would have guessed her fear. There were plenty of risks inherent in her career, but those were easy ones to take. Or they had been until that turned personal as well.

Now she was left in limbo, needing to go but wanting to stay. That wanting was the most terrifying thing she could imagine.

She straightened as voices echoed from the path behind her. Voices she recognized.

"What are you doing here?" she asked as Tessa, Madison and Cory appeared in the clearing. Tessa carried a picnic basket while Cory had a quilt draped over one arm and Madison hefted a cooler in her arms. Tonight had been a Chop It Like It's Hot meeting, although they'd planned to munch on appetizers and do a mini-bachelorette celebration for Tessa.

At this point, the cooking club was just an excuse to get together. These three women had truly become her best friends. But she'd sent a text earlier saying she had a headache and would see them on Saturday at the wedding. There wasn't a chance she would let her melancholy bring down the mood of the group.

"You can't ghost us," Madison said in her normal commanding tone. "That isn't done as part of cooking club. It's a rule."

"There are no rules," Ella countered, coming to her feet. "How did you even find me?"

Tessa wrinkled her nose. "I might have put you in find my phone that one time when I was looking at a recipe on yours."

Ella blinked. "You track me?"

"Not actively," Tessa said, blushing. "But I wanted to have it for when you leave town. You know, in case there's ever an emergency."

Cory didn't bother to hide her smile. "It's weird, but if it makes you feel better, she's tracking us, too."

"I care about you guys, okay?" Tessa had gone

beet red, her cheeks nearly the color of her flaming hair. "You are my family in all the ways that count, and I look after my family. I promise I only look in emergencies."

"Tonight was an emergency?" Ella asked. She wasn't mad. In a strange way, it was kind of sweet that Tessa checked in on them.

Tessa had lived a fairly sheltered life, suffering from a severe kidney condition since she was a kid. A successful transplant a few years ago had changed things. Out of all of them, she was the most inherently cautious, even though she liked to think of herself as a rebel.

Tessa's idea of rebellion might have been crossing an empty street on a don't-walk sign.

"Plus, you can't be mad at me because I'm the bride. My wedding is in a couple of days, and I think I should get a pass."

Ella raised a brow. "I'm disturbed but not angry."

Tessa dropped the picnic basket to the ground and enveloped Ella in a tight hug. "Thank you. I can live with disturbed."

Cory joined them, but when she gestured to Madison, the cool blonde shook her head.

"This moment is not hug-worthy," she said, then glared at Ella. "Because I'm mad at you."

"Me? I'm not the one tracking your whereabouts."

"You canceled on cooking club without a good excuse, and I made homemade spanakopita in honor of us celebrating the bride-to-be. It's a labor-intensive recipe."

"I'm sure it's great," Ella said. Madison remained the tiniest bit terrifying to her.

"Sit down." Madison pointed a finger at the ground. "Cory, spread that blanket. Before we dive further into why this one—" she inclined her chin toward Ella "—faked a headache, we're going to eat. Otherwise, I'll be hangry. I'm not that nice when I'm hangry."

"You're not that nice when you're full," Ella muttered. "And I didn't fake the headache. My head hurts."

Her heart hurt worse, but why get into that?

"Good food will make it better," Madison answered.

"I love this statue of your mom," Cory said as they unpacked the picnic basket and the bottle of wine from the cooler along with four plastic cups. "I didn't know her, obviously, but somehow I feel like I understand how amazing she was just from this."

"She was that amazing and more." Ella coughed to cover the tremble in her voice. "I thought it was stupid when my dad told me he was having this statue built, but I've taken to coming here to visit with her while I've been home. I feel bad that it took me until this summer... I feel bad about a lot of things. This place helps me feel better."

"It's always better late than never to pull your head out of...well, you know," Cory confirmed.

Ella managed a smile, although she was less likely than her friends to let herself off the hook. "I guess."

She took the cup Tessa handed her. "Oh, I forgot to tell you, the ribbon and fabric for the ceremony arbor arrived at camp today. I stored everything in the nurse's office to make sure it would stay safe. We're all meeting tomorrow afternoon to decorate, right?"

Tessa beamed. "Yes, and I cannot wait. Mostly I can't wait to be finished with all of this. Unlike Cory, craft projects aren't my favorite. I'm so nervous about my family being here, and it's strange for me to be in the position of the one worrying."

"I can help with any last-minute crafting," Cory promised. "Your family is going to be thrilled at how happy and healthy you are. There's nothing to worry about."

Tessa made a face. "Easy for you to say now that you're happily married. I feel like I'm turning into a bridezilla with all of my stress. Sometimes Carson and Lauren look at me like I have a horn growing out of my head with the weird stuff that comes out of my mouth these days."

The knot in Ella's stomach unwound slightly at Tessa's description of her fiancé and his ten-year-old daughter, both of whom adored her. Why had she thought about canceling and not seeing her friends tonight? They always made her feel happy and loved, even in her darkest moods. They did that for each other.

"You couldn't be a bridezilla if you tried," Madison said. "The only horn you'd sprout is that of a unicorn with sparkles and rainbows. But if you're worried about it, start delegating. We can all help."

They discussed the wedding and who would step in to run interference with Tessa's overprotective parents if the need arose. The longer they ate, the more relaxed Ella became. Every now and again, she glanced up at the bronze statue.

Her mother would have liked these women. She would have appreciated the role they played in Ella's life.

"Now that we've dealt with the last-minute bride nonemergencies, it's time to turn our attention to the real issue." Ella cringed as Madison's sharp gaze landed on her.

"I'm not an issue. There's no issue."

Her three friends continued to study her with varying looks of sympathy and irritation—the irritation mostly from Madison.

"Kayla has asked me to help with a weekend event for pediatric cancer patients and their families."

"You're perfect for that," Tessa said.

Cory nodded. "You do have experience."

"But you don't want to get involved," Madison guessed.

"It's scheduled for the weekend after the wedding, right before I'm supposed to leave. I know what she's doing. She's trying to suck me in and make me feel committed to staying."

"Would that be the only reason you'd consider staying?" Madison raised a brow. "It doesn't have anything to do with the hot single dad you're sleeping with?"

Tessa and Cory let out twin gasps of surprise.

"Hot single dad as in Josh? And what do you mean sleeping with?" Cory demanded. "Since when did that happen?"

"I don't know what you're talking about," Ella told Madison, doing her best to sound both amused and affronted and not like she was desperately panicking on the inside. Nobody knew about her and Josh.

Certainly, he wouldn't have told anyone. His friends had connections all over town, but she didn't believe he would have shared that information. And if he had...

"I don't sleep much," Madison said calmly. "Sometimes I take walks in the wee hours. The other night I was walking past Josh's house and happened to see you leaving. It was four in the morning, and you looked tousled and happy. I never look happy at that time unless—"

"It was... I was... It's complicated."

"Great sex isn't complicated," Madison argued, "unless there's something more to it than sex."

"She means if you like him," Tessa clarified.

Ella gave the barest hint of a nod. "I know what she means."

"Do you?" Cory asked. "Do you like Josh?"

"Everybody likes Josh." Ella's laugh sounded only the tiniest bit hysterical. "What's not to like?"

"For one thing, the fact that he's here and you're still planning to leave in a couple of weeks," Madison suggested. "You could not like that."

"It's not a big deal. We both knew what was happening."

"Are you sure about that?" Cory placed a hand on Ella's leg and squeezed. "Because Josh isn't the type of guy to do things casually."

"Not usually." Ella began packing up leftover food. "He's different with me. I'm not the kind of person he'd consider seriously, and he's not my type at all."

"Right." Madison sniffed. "Handsome, stable and kind are big turnoffs."

Ella turned to Tessa, needing somebody to understand what she was trying to say, even if it barely made sense in her mind. "Remember when you decided you wanted some excitement in your life, and Carson was the guy to give it to you? That's how it is for Josh and me. I know I'm not right for him, so it was easy to…" She wiggled her hands in front of her face. "You know, because it didn't have to mean anything. It doesn't mean anything."

"He's bringing Crystal to the wedding," Tessa said on a rush of breath.

"That's great," Ella murmured, even though the news gave her an emotional jolt. She focused on cleanup and picking up the blanket to fold as they all stood, hoping no one could see her quivering fingers. "Josh has a girlfriend. That's one more thing checked off my list before I leave."

"Great sex or finding a girlfriend for the man you're having sex with?" Madison didn't look convinced.

"It sounds bad when you say it like that, but Josh and I have an understanding. This is what I want."

She had a feeling that none of her friends was deceived by the lie, but she wasn't going to reveal anything more. She wanted this, no matter what her heart told her.

Chapter Eighteen

Josh tugged at his collar as he watched Carson and Tessa exchange vows looking over the lake at Tall Pines Camp the following Saturday. He'd been to several weddings since his divorce, but the celebration today affected him in ways he couldn't explain and definitely did not like.

Anna jumped up from the bench where she sat next to him as the ceremony ended, ready to toss flower petals at the newly married couple.

His gaze collided with Ella's, and he flashed a small smile. The one she returned resembled a grimace more than a grin, but he couldn't blame her when he had a date standing on his other side. Ella stood between Madison and Cory as if her friends were somehow protecting her, which was a ridiculous thought. If any person could fend for themselves, it would be Ella. She was strong, fiercely independent and had made it clear she didn't need anyone, particularly him.

He'd thought about canceling with Crystal and not bringing a date to the wedding. At this point, he didn't know what had possessed him to invite her in the first place. Probably the feeling of desperation he got as a result of his confusion about his relationship with Ella.

She was leaving. Nothing had changed even though his heart held so much affection… No, that was a cowardly word to use. He loved her. He was in love with a woman who did not want a future with him. She did not want to be part of the life he had.

Of course, he'd invited Crystal to the wedding. He was surrounded by his friends. Tessa and Carson were both new to Starlight, but they had a close-knit group, and Josh knew almost every guest at the hundred-person reception by name.

And they were all watching him. Poor Josh whose father had never approved of him, whose daughter had been sick and whose wife had left him. Pathetic Josh who'd needed his brother to help him make his first real business venture a success.

In his rational mind, he knew those things weren't all that made him who he was, but right now, it sure felt that way. He felt different with Ella. He felt like a stronger version of himself and liked that version.

He wanted to keep going but didn't know how to maintain it without her.

"I'm gonna go find Evie," Anna said as they began to walk toward the converted barn where the reception would take place.

"Did you get a little teary during the ceremony?" Crystal asked in her kind voice. "I have to admit I cried. Weddings always make me emotional."

Anna looked at the woman like she was speaking a foreign language. "No, I didn't cry."

Josh placed a hand on his daughter's shoulder. "I don't think Anna is quite at the age to get emotional about people vowing to spend the rest of their lives together."

Anna shook her head like he'd lost his mind as well, then shrugged away from his touch to find her friend.

"Normally kids like me," Crystal said, clearly picking up on his daughter's attitude. "My nieces and nephews and their friends call me f-ant."

Josh wasn't sure if it was his brain or his general exhaustion at this point, but he couldn't make sense of the moniker. "Why do they call you that?"

"Fun aunt," she explained. "F-ant. Sort of like the soda without an extra a."

"Makes sense," he agreed. "Let's get a drink."

They joined Parker and Mara as well as Kaitlyn and Finn, who were standing near the bar situated in one corner of the barn.

"You did a great job with this place," Parker said.

"We used to come up here in high school for parties. It was a mess back then."

"Thanks," Josh said. "I never came to the camp for parties." He had never been much of a partier. Not much for adventure in any form until he'd met Ella.

"Evie tells us you're getting a dog?" Mara gave him a smug smile. "This is a new development."

Josh cringed. "Anna was broken up over a stray we found. She was hoping we could end up adopting him, but his family was waiting. I figure I've put off the inevitable long enough."

"That's so sweet," Crystal said. "She's lucky to have such a bighearted daddy."

He appreciated the compliment. At least he was trying to. Ella would have called him a pushover again, and they would have laughed about his devotion to Anna. Josh missed laughing with Ella.

Was it possible to miss things he hadn't even experienced yet? That's how he felt about her leaving. He'd never spent a Halloween with her or Christmas, but he missed seeing her nose with the red tip as they skated around a local ice rink or cuddled up in front of the fire after a day of sledding. He and Anna had made their own traditions, after Jenn left. And he wanted to share them with Ella. Only Ella.

"Be sure to look for one that's hypoallergenic," Crystal said, giving his hand a squeeze. "I'm allergic."

There was a ripple of silent conversation among his friends so subtle that his date for the evening didn't pick up on it. Then Parker raised a brow in Josh's direction.

"I'll remember that," Josh told his date, unsure of how else to answer.

Operation Date My Dad or whatever they'd named it was a colossal flop. He'd fallen for the wrong woman.

Wrong in every way, but somehow right for him.

He did his best to avoid being close to Ella the rest of the evening and had a feeling she was doing the same.

She danced with her friends and her brother. At one point, she and Anna were the final two contestants in a limbo contest. It made his heart ache to watch his daughter laughing with the woman who would not be a part of their future.

Josh excused himself from Crystal and his friends, then walked out into the cool night. Stars dotted the clear sky, and he heard water ripple in gentle laps against the shore.

These mountains were his home, and they had been since the day he was born. Now it felt inevitable that to claim his life, he'd have to leave everything he'd known. He needed a new start in a place where he didn't have a history and every memory wasn't colored by the past.

He turned at the sound of laughter behind him and saw Ella and Madison emerge from the barn. The prickly—if talented—chef spotted him first.

She gave Ella a nudge then disappeared back into the reception.

Ella's gaze softened for the briefest second before clouding over as she approached him. "Your kid cheats at limbo," she announced.

"First, you were beaten by an eight-year-old," he returned, "and now you've got to throw her under the bus. Way to be a sore loser."

He almost apologized for the words as soon as they were out of his mouth. They were so different from what he would typically say to someone in this instance.

Ella lifted her gaze to the sky and let out a throaty chuckle, never failing to surprise him. "Okay, she didn't cheat. But I've never lost a limbo contest before now. I had a reputation to protect."

"I have a feeling Anna isn't a threat to your reputation."

Her full lips pressed together. "Nice work on bringing a date. I'm just sorry I didn't find her for you. I feel like I shirked my duty."

There were no words to express how much he didn't want to talk about his dating life with Ella. He'd already decided that he would end things with Crystal after tonight. The decision had less to do with Ella or even Anna, although perhaps his daughter wasn't as ready for him to start dating as she'd led all of them to believe.

Knowing Ella was walking away didn't change his feelings for her. As was Josh's pattern, he couldn't stop himself from craving the affection of a person unwilling to give it to him.

He imagined some psychological lesson he could learn from this. Something about choosing people who were emotionally unavailable or repeating the relationship dynamic he'd had with his father.

But no deep insight was going to change his feelings about it.

He'd rather be alone than with the wrong person.

He glanced over as Crystal stepped out of the barn. "Everything okay?" she asked with that gentle smile that made him feel like the biggest jerk in the world. "You've been gone awhile."

"Just getting a little fresh air," Josh said, taking a step around Ella.

"Nice limbo moves," Crystal said. "I don't think we've met."

If Josh had his tool belt on at the moment, he'd grab a hammer from it and knock himself out. Instead, he acted like a grown-up and introduced Crystal to Ella.

"You two make a cute couple," Ella said. He clenched his jaw so hard he thought his teeth might crack.

"Thanks." Crystal took his hand. "I was nervous to meet Josh's friends tonight, but everyone is just as nice as him."

"I'm not nice," Ella said calmly. "Ask anyone." She laughed. "Ask Anna."

Crystal grimaced. "Anna and I aren't quite close

friends yet. I think it's difficult to come to terms with another woman in her daddy's life. But we'll get there."

"Yeah," Ella said slowly. She gave Josh a questioning glance, and he tried not to squirm.

He was still wrapping his mind around the idea that it had been his daughter's idea for him to find a girlfriend, but she seemed to want nothing to do with one who embodied everything they should both want. Not that he had any room to talk.

"Change is often an adjustment," he said, wondering if the words sounded as imbecilic out loud as they did in his head. Of course change was an adjustment, by definition.

"So true," Crystal agreed with a heartfelt nod.

"You might want to cross-stitch that bit of wisdom onto a throw pillow," Ella suggested with a snort. "Nice to meet you, Crystal. Hope you two have a good night."

Then she turned for the reception and Josh was left watching the one person he knew he wanted walk away.

Ella smiled as the group of kids started through the obstacle course Rob had fashioned in the front yard outside the main cabin the following weekend, a few intrepid parents following.

"This event is a huge success," Kayla said as she put an arm around Ella's shoulder. "It was last-minute, but that works best sometimes. You're part of what's making it great."

"I'm giving out stickers and listening to parents talk about their kids." Ella rolled her eyes. "Not exactly expert stuff."

Kayla squeezed Ella's arm. "You are a professional and a sympathetic ear. It's important."

"Did you create this entire event to prove a point to me?" She wasn't sure whether to feel irritated or grateful.

"This is a worthy cause, and we're happy to support it." Kayla shrugged. "Just like you always have our support. I wish I could change the past. I wish I could make it so that you felt less alone when your mom died. I wish you would change your mind about leaving, but most of all, I hope you finally learn to see your own worth."

"Ditto what she said."

Ella turned in surprise at the sound of her father's deep voice.

Jack wore an olive green polo shirt and tan pants with sneakers, casual by her father's standards. "I hope it's okay that I'm here?"

She nodded, surprised to discover that she was truly happy to see him. "Sure."

Her dad let out a long sigh. "I'm blown away by these kids and their families, the way they keep hoping and believing."

Ella hugged him. Hope was a double-edged sword

as far as she was concerned. She wanted to believe in it but trusting felt like too high a risk to take.

As Dr. Steadman gathered everyone toward the picnic area and announced the weekend's final speaker, Ella's head snapped up to stare at Kayla.

The older woman had the good sense to look vaguely embarrassed. "We needed somebody who'd successfully overcome what many of these kids are dealing with. Like your dad said, we need more hope."

Ella's heart began to pound, and she released her father. She hadn't spoken to Josh since the wedding. He'd finished the projects he was working on at the camp to focus on the partnership with the California company. Ella had heard from Cory that Josh planned to sign the deal.

Their gazes met, and he gave her the kind of distant smile a person would offer to a casual acquaintance. Anna's eyes narrowed, and the girl looked away, ready to do her best to ignore Ella.

Ella respected her for that, although she was intensely curious as to why Anna found fault with Josh's sensible potential girlfriend. She would have expected her to at least give the woman a chance. But a secret, selfish part of her was happy the girl didn't approve, although she knew that spoke badly of her.

"I also thought this might be an opportunity for you to talk with him." Kayla leaned in and wiggled her eyebrows. "By talk, I mean make up."

"Kayla." Ella sighed. "This isn't going to work. Josh and I are not a couple."

Her mother's friend shrugged. "I think the two of you are the only ones who believe that."

"He has a girlfriend now, or at least a woman he's dating. He's moving on with his life, and so am I."

"That's not what I heard. I heard he ended things the night of Tessa's wedding."

Ella frowned. She hadn't heard that. Why hadn't anyone told her? "It still doesn't matter. I'm leaving."

"Have you signed the contract?" Kayla asked softly.

"I'm going to need to separate the two of you," Ella said, flicking a glance between Kayla and her father. "He's the only one who knows I still haven't signed."

"We're worried about you," Jack said, at least having the good grace to appear sheepish.

"We have a few last-minute details to work out," Ella explained to them both. "I'm heading to the Traveling Nurses office in San Francisco before my first assignment. I'll sign everything in person."

"The answer is no?" Kayla looked pleased. "You don't have a contract."

"I'm going to sign." She couldn't explain what had stopped her to this point, but it felt reasonable and rational to wait and sign in person. She liked feeling reasonable and rational.

"Still no," Kayla insisted.

Ella knew Kayla meant well. She tried to smile,

but her face felt frozen. Her whole body seemed to be made of ice, particularly her heart. It was a defense mechanism. She recognized it and didn't try to stop the sensation.

Josh followed his daughter to the front of the picnic area where the families had gathered to listen to Dr. Steadman speak.

Ella's heart felt like it might actually crack in two as the doctor introduced Josh and Anna to the crowd.

Josh stepped forward and began to recount Anna's history, from the first sign of unexplained leg pain to the battery of tests that had led to her diagnosis and then her treatment and what that had cost both Anna and their family.

He didn't gloss over the fact that his wife had left but admitted how difficult that time had been and gave suggestions to the parents watching of how to support each other. He took responsibility for the way he'd dealt with the pressure and for some of the troubles in his marriage.

Next, he spoke directly to the men in the audience, and Ella could see several of them shift uncomfortably as his words urging them to stay involved obviously hit home. Then he asked Anna to say a few words.

Ella had never been prouder of anyone in her entire life as she was of that eight-year-old girl as she made both the parents and kids in the audience laugh and, in several cases, reduced them to tears as she talked about what having cancer meant to her. The two of them and their bravery left Ella feeling like the worst sort of coward.

She hadn't been fooling anyone about her reasons for staying in Starlight. And to have Josh and Anna's courage and strength on such clear display shamed her. Her mother would have been disappointed, which was the worst of all.

She'd let fear run her life, keep her running away for far too long. There were no guarantees, but this summer had finally taught her that trying to make her life seem like an adventure from the outside didn't make her feel brave on the inside.

Accepting her emotions and being vulnerable first with Josh and then as she worked on repairing her relationship with her dad had given Ella her most gratifying feelings of satisfaction and strength.

Josh took over speaking again, and she looked around at the crowd. One reason she'd been afraid to consider settling down was what it would mean to really get to know her patients on a long-term basis.

As a traveling nurse, she could more easily keep her emotional distance, at least that's what she'd tried to convince herself. In reality, she cared about every one of her patients like they were members of her own family. She finally understood that made her stronger, not weaker. Josh and Anna made her stronger.

The realization sent a burst of energy zinging through her. She knew what she wanted. Now she needed to convince the two of them to give her a chance to prove it.

A thunderous round of applause from the audience snapped her attention back to the present. Dr. Steadman was shaking Josh's hand. Anna smiled as well, but to Ella, it looked as if she were about to be sick to her stomach.

She turned to Kayla. "What did I miss? What happened?"

"Did you know?" the older woman asked. "Is that why you won't consider staying?"

"What are you talking about? What did Josh say?" Ella glanced around furtively as the gathered crowd began to disperse.

"Josh announced that he and Anna are moving to California."

Ella swallowed. "No." She shook her head, unsure whether she answered Kayla's question or expressed her feelings on the announcement. Either way, the word *no* continued to echo in her brain.

He'd decided without telling her. Not that he owed her anything, but it hurt. She didn't have a lot of time to process the news as a few people from the hospital approached and asked about her plans.

"I'm leaving," she said. More than ever, the words sounded hollow. She felt hollow. It was ridiculous. Josh and Anna didn't belong to her.

She'd been planning to leave up until a couple of minutes ago. She excused herself and headed back to the main cabin and the quiet solitude of the nurse's office. She needed a moment to collect herself and digest this abrupt change.

She shouldn't be as upset as she was. This was about Josh's life and didn't have anything to do with her.

But some secret, embarrassing part of her had wanted Josh to fight. Like her life was a cheesy '80s romance. He'd stand outside her rental with a boom box blaring to let her know how much he cared. He'd do anything. Say anything.

And she would finally be able to risk her heart because she would know it was safe with him. But she wasn't safe. She was inextricably heartbroken, and the worst part was she had no right to be.

She looked up from her desk when the door opened.

"You messed everything up," Anna said, her voice quavering with anger. "You were supposed to find somebody for him so he would be happy here, and now he's leaving. We're leaving. It's all your fault."

"Anna, I'm sorry," Ella said. "But I don't think I have anything to do with your dad's decision to leave Starlight."

"Yes, you do. He couldn't fall for any of the women he tried to date because of you."

"Because of me?" Ella stood and came around the desk. "Your dad brought a date to Tessa's wedding. But he told me you didn't like her. So who exactly is influencing him?"

"She's allergic to dogs," Anna said as if that explained everything. "Now we're moving to California so we can get a dog."

Ella blinked, trying to follow the girl's train of thought.

"Well, you wanted a dog so that's great, right?"

"I should have never made that deal with you. I should have known you would mess everything up."

"I still don't see—"

"Because he likes you. You were supposed to find somebody nice for him. Instead he likes you, and you aren't nice. You are leaving."

The words felt like flames being shot directly at Ella's frozen heart, painfully bringing it back to life and making her wish for the cold once again.

"That isn't what happened," she said, unsure which of them she was trying to convince.

"I hate you," Anna said. "I wish you would have never come back to this town. I wish I hadn't gone to visit your mom's stupid statue. She's probably happy that accident—"

"Anna, enough." Josh's voice was fiercer than Ella had imagined it could be.

But it wasn't enough. She knew where Anna had been going with that sentence. It spoke to her greatest fear—that somehow she deserved to lose her mother. She deserved to be rejected or abandoned by anyone she truly loved.

"Apologize," Josh commanded his daughter. "The idea to move was mine. And you will make friends in California just like you have friends here. But I need this, sweetheart. I need a change right now."

Anna swallowed. Once again, Ella gave the kid props for her strength. She glared at Ella. "I'm sorry," she said through clenched teeth. "I'm sorry you messed it all up." Then she turned and ran from the room.

Chapter Nineteen

Josh watched emotions play across Ella's delicate features that he would never have expected to see there in response to him or his daughter. Regret, sorrow, heartbreak.

None of it made sense.

She was leaving. She'd made that abundantly clear. Had her decision factored into his?

Maybe.

Definitely.

He wouldn't apologize for that, but what had seemed like the right solution for taking control of his life even an hour ago now made him feel like he'd made a colossal mistake. Josh had devoted everything to Anna, and he thought that at least in parenting, he could feel confident in his choices.

"I don't understand," he muttered, running a hand through his hair. "When I talked to her about it, she seemed excited. She was ready for a change as long as we could adopt a dog when we got there. She's strong. She's resilient. She never wavers. And now..."

He met Ella's still-stunned gaze and shook his head. "Did you say something to her?"

"Do you really believe that? What do you think of me, Josh?"

"I don't know what to think."

Her eyes lowered to the ground before returning to him. "What if I told you I want to stay?"

His stomach felt like it dropped to his toes. "It's too late," he said before his foolish heart could believe her.

"Too late," she countered. "I think I'm in love with you."

"No." He shook his head. "You aren't. You can't be. I told you how I felt, and you responded like I was a bug on the bottom of your shoe."

She cringed. "I don't think it was quite like that."

"It felt a lot exactly like that," he told her. "And not my first rodeo as the bug. You've ruined me for other women, Ella. There's a good chance you've ruined this town for me as well. I've lived here my whole life. Now I see you in everything. Things we did. Things I'd like to do with you."

He leaned toward her. "At this moment, I can't

imagine a single one that either of us would enjoy. I don't trust you not to break my heart."

"I wouldn't—"

"Sure you would, because I'm not worth the effort," he said, not bothering to keep the frustration out of his voice. "There's nothing special or exciting about me. I'm not worth the effort."

"Josh, no."

"My dad started teaching me that lesson, and my ex-wife pretty much finished the job. But their rejection and abandonment would be the icing on the cake compared to—"

"I'm not rejecting you." Ella lifted a hand, but he stepped away.

"I won't give you the chance. I know how this works. You say the right words now, and I try to become the person you want me to be. The guy who's going to make you happy. When I fail, you pick up and leave. I'm left behind. Again. To be the laughing-stock of Starlight once more. Poor Josh."

She shook her head. "That's not going to happen. I don't want you to change. I just want you." The words were like a straight shot to his heart. "I want to make a life with you and Anna. Please give us a chance."

He wanted to trust her. His heart begged to take the risk, but it was too much. The stakes felt too high. What would it do to him if he let Ella in all the way—and he understood the depth of his feelings for her—and she hurt him?

He'd be left alone, but it wasn't just about him. Anna was part of this, and she'd already been through too much. He could deal with his daughter being mad, but he wasn't sure how he'd handle it if he saw disappointment in her sweet eyes. If she saw him as a failure. "I can't do this. Not given what it could mean."

"Josh, please. At least—"

He shook his head and tried to find the right words despite the battle warring inside him. He wanted to pull Ella into his arms and never let her go. It was his father's voice ringing through Josh's head that stopped him.

The refrain of Josh being needy and pathetic. He'd heard it so many times, and even though the rational part of his brain knew those emotional jabs had been his dad's way of controlling him, resulting in more pain than his dad's fists could ever deliver, Josh couldn't deny the truth in them.

"Good luck, Ella. With wherever life takes you next."

Unable to continue facing the look of sorry in her gaze, he turned and walked away.

Ella returned to her mother's statue every day that week.

Cory and Madison continually checked in on her because they were the only ones who knew that she'd put her heart on the line for Josh and he'd rejected her. Tessa had even texted from her honeymoon, and

Ella did her level best to convince her friends as well as herself that she was okay.

She would be okay. She'd dealt with more significant losses than Josh, but her heart wasn't getting the message quite yet. His rejection was terrible enough, but Anna's anger had gutted her.

She'd not only let the girl down, but in doing so, had failed in her quest to honor her mother's memory. Nothing seemed to ease that sting.

"I'm glad to see you here," her father said from behind her.

Ella turned and offered him a weak smile. "It makes me feel close to her."

"I wasn't sure when I first commissioned this statue if it was the right thing to do," he told her. "Part of me felt like it was indulging my grief, and I should mourn your mother privately."

Ella's chest tightened at the wistful look in her dad's eyes as he stared at the bronze likeness of her mom. Jack was dating a wonderful woman at this point, and Ella had wondered if he'd finally gotten over his wife's death. Sometimes it seemed like she was the only member of her family left grappling with the past.

She now understood that wasn't true. And it did her no good to continue believing she was alone.

"Mom would have loved this," she said gently. "It would have made her happy to bring joy and comfort to people the way this statue obviously does.

It's a good thing. I'm sorry it took me so long to realize that."

He reached out and wrapped her in a tight hug. "Ella, you never have to apologize to me. I wish things had been different in the past, but I'm grateful for where we are now."

"Me, too, Dad."

"You know I'm on the hospital board of directors. The town's nursing shortage remains all too real."

She shook her head. "I've made a commitment. What would it say about me if I backed out now?"

"It would say you had a change of heart. Don't make other people's opinions more important. You're the one who matters."

Ella almost laughed at that. It felt like she'd waited her whole life for her father to say those words. Maybe she should be embarrassed as an adult woman to want and need that support. It was enough that they were finally in a place where he could offer, and she could accept it.

"I always thought I had to leave this town to find happiness and success in life. If I stayed, Mom's memory and my stupid destructive patterns would sink me." She rolled her eyes. "Turns out, I could sink five thousand miles away just as easily."

"You didn't sink, sweetheart. You're here."

"I've wasted so much time, Dad. With you and my life and…"

"With your heart," he guessed.

She pointed at him. "I'm not sure I can deal with

this new, insightful Jack Samuelson. It's a little disturbing."

"You know how Kayla likes to talk. She cares about you like you're one of her kids. Even if I hadn't been aware of what was going on between you and that Johnson boy, she would have made sure I was kept in the loop."

"He's not a boy, Dad."

"I know that. From all accounts, he's a good man. Both Josh and his brother. I wish I'd paid more attention to what was going on in that family." Jack inclined his head. "I believed what Mac Johnson wanted people to believe. I could have done something if I'd realized."

He massaged a hand over his face. "Who am I kidding? I couldn't even handle my own two kids after your mother died. I would have been useless in helping anyone else. I'm not the rescuing type."

"Maybe not," Ella agreed. "Despite everything that happened, maybe it was more important that Finn and I learned to be strong enough to rescue ourselves. I can't promise anything, Dad. I'm not supposed to leave for San Francisco until this weekend. I'll set up a meeting with Eric Steadman before I go and see what he has to say. Maybe I'm done running after all."

"Whatever you choose, know that you always have a home here. That will never change."

Her father glanced at his watch. "I'm meeting

your brother and Kaitlyn for dinner. Do you want to join us?"

She shook her head. "I'm going to stay with Mom for another couple of minutes."

They said their goodbyes, and Ella lowered herself to the ground when she was alone again. Her heart was still sore from the conversation with Josh, but a little bit of gladness poked through all the sorrow. Closing her eyes, she breathed deeply for the first time in a long while. Maybe she could finally accept that she was home.

"Why don't you love my daddy?"

Ella opened her eyes and stared up at Anna leaning over her, hands on hips and eyes flashing.

"I don't think that's an appropriate question," Ella told the girl even as she searched for a way to answer.

"He loves you, and he's the best."

"Not arguing that point." Ella sat up and looked past Anna. "Shouldn't you be at soccer practice?"

"I needed a potty break."

Ella made a show of glancing around the garden space. "You took a wrong turn."

"If you loved him, we wouldn't have to move to California."

"For the record, I told your father I loved him, and he's still planning to move." She studied the young girl. "He thought you were okay with it until that scene in my office."

"I thought I was," Anna said bitterly. "But I'm not."

"If it makes you feel any better, I'm not a big fan of you moving either."

"What do you care when you're leaving?"

"I've changed my mind."

Anna stomped her cleated foot. "No fair. You get to stay, and I have to move away."

"You get a dog."

"I don't want—" Anna drew in a shaky breath. "We can adopt a dog in Starlight. We already have a fenced backyard and everything."

"Why do you want me to love your dad, anyway?" Ella drew her knees up to her chest and leaned forward. "I thought you didn't like me."

"I like you okay. At least you aren't allergic to dogs."

"I'm sorry about Grover, sweetie. I never had a chance to tell you that. But he's happy to be back with his regular family, and so that leaves you available to rescue a different dog in need of a good home."

"But not one who lives in California," Anna insisted.

"Admit it." Ella reached out and poked a finger into the girl's tiny belly. "I have more positive traits than liking dogs. You kind of have a thing for me."

"You don't wear too much perfume or talk baby talk to me." Anna crossed her arms over her chest. "Am I the reason you won't love my daddy? Because I could get sick again? I promise I'll try not to."

Ella felt like she'd taken a punch to the gut. "I love both you and your dad, Anna. I didn't want to, but

I do." She bit down on her lip and then continued, "Part of my fear had to do with your illness, but it wasn't because I was afraid of you getting sick. I'm a nurse. I'm good at dealing with sick people."

"Then why?"

"I'm afraid of losing another person I love."

"I feel that way, too." Anna glanced at the statue of Katie Samuelson as she spoke. Ella felt humbled by the girl's words. Of course a child would feel that way. Anna's mother had walked away when things got hard. She was still a part of her life, but that was almost more of a rejection than Ella had suffered. Ella knew there was no way her mother would have left if she'd had the choice.

Katie would have fought tooth and nail to stay with her family. Ella might not have her mother's innate sweetness, but she could channel her strength and fight for the life she wanted the way her mom would have.

She got to her feet and pointed at Anna. "Just so we're clear, I love you and you love me."

Anna considered the statement for so long it almost made Ella laugh out loud. "Yes," the girl agreed finally.

"And we both love your father."

"Because he's the best."

Ella nodded. "The very best. He's absolutely devoted to you, so now we need to convince him that he can't live without me." The words gave Ella a funny feeling in her stomach.

She'd never tried advocating for herself or risking her heart in the way it would take to convince Josh to give her another chance. She wasn't going to let him or Anna go without a fight. That much she knew for certain.

"I think we can do it," Anna said, "but it has to be fast. He wants to move before school starts."

Ella thought about that. "Then we'll work quickly," she promised the girl. "He doesn't stand a chance with the two of us working together."

She started to give Anna a hug, then pulled back. Instead, she opened her palm, spit on the center and held out her hand. "Seems to me that we've got a new deal," she told the girl.

Anna grinned and took Ella's hand, shaking it with exaggerated motions. "We've got a deal," she confirmed, "but I've got to get back to practice."

"We'll figure out the details," Ella promised. "This is going to work, Anna."

The girl nodded. "It has to."

Chapter Twenty

Josh sighed as he took in the valley below on the drive up the pass to Tall Pines two days later. He'd driven this stretch of road dozens of times, maybe more, but today the view seemed to hold special meaning.

It might be the last time he appreciated the beauty before he and Anna left for California. They were scheduled to begin the two-day trip in a little over a week, and anxiety had taken over as his go-to emotion.

He had no idea if he was doing the right thing for himself or his daughter. In fact, the closer they got to the departure date, the more he doubted his decision.

He'd rented a fully furnished duplex for the first

six months and would keep his house in Starlight until then because that felt like a more manageable commitment. Parker had reminded Josh several times that he could partner with the California-based development company without relocating.

It had come as a shock to everyone that Josh would consider moving. At the time he'd had the conversation with the company's CEO, it seemed like a good idea—a way to start fresh and forge a brand-new path.

But was he just avoiding his issues by moving?

He wanted to believe it would all work out, but there were no guarantees. He passed the stretch of road where he and Anna had found Ella searching for the stray dog, a needed reminder of why this change was for the best.

His heart still reeled after Ella's declaration to him the previous weekend, and that made him know he had to get away.

How could he stay with memories of his time with her clinging to him like intrepid vines? Had he done the right thing pushing her away? Long, restless nights with very little sleep told him no.

Yet he'd trusted her with his heart, and she'd ultimately rejected him in the same way he'd been discarded too many times in the past. Josh had always been the one to put himself on the line for the people he loved, and mostly he'd been left disappointed and heartbroken.

Ella wasn't any different, or so he told himself.

Maybe her change of heart was real, but the risk of being emotionally gutted was too much for him to take a chance on it.

He forced himself to concentrate on the drive and not the mountains he loved and might always consider home.

There were mountains in California, maybe not as close as he preferred, but he'd find his place somewhere new.

Wouldn't he?

Before he could think better of it, Josh pulled to the side of the road and climbed out of the truck. His chest rose and fell in deep gasps of air like he'd just run a marathon.

He moved to the edge of the road where it dropped off down the hill. A warm breeze lifted from the valley, and he studied the town below him. Starlight. The only home he'd ever known.

The only home he wanted.

The realization hit him like that jump into the cold lake with Ella. He didn't want to leave this place. It felt like he'd had no choice to prove he could make it despite his father's opinion about him, but that was the scared, hurt boy inside him talking.

Josh was a man now, and he had choices. He had the power. Nothing could take that from him, especially not his father's memory.

He didn't need to start over or run away to claim his freedom from the past. He just needed to be willing to reach for it.

With shaky fingers, he pulled the phone from his back pocket and dialed the number of the development company. After weeks of worrying and planning, it took less than five minutes for Josh to work out a deal with the CEO that would be right for both of them.

Josh would manage a three-state region and consult on any mixed-use redevelopment projects, but he'd keep his home base in Starlight.

His home.

It still hurt to think that Ella wouldn't be a part of it, but he knew she'd left two days earlier for her new future. Regret was a harsh mistress, and it weighed on his heart.

He didn't want to hold her back, but maybe he could reach out in a few weeks and explain that his fear had colored his last conversation with her. Maybe if she knew he was a sure thing, she'd be willing to give him another chance.

It grated to think that he might not be worth more than a sure thing to her, but the truth remained that he was deeply in love with her. That wouldn't change.

Sometimes love meant compromise, even if his feelings were stronger than hers.

He got back in his truck and drove the rest of the way to camp. Anna and Evie were waiting in the parking lot when he pulled in.

The summer sessions had wrapped up in anticipation of school starting, but Kayla had asked if the girls would spend the day at camp. She'd had a photographer and videographer booked to get some footage for a new marketing campaign in which his daughter and her best friend were thrilled to participate.

"How was your starring role? Are the two of you headed to Hollywood anytime soon?" he asked as he got out of the truck.

Evie shook her head.

"I hate California," Anna said decisively.

"As a matter of fact…" Josh crouched down in front of his girl. "I had a phone call with the development company. We've worked out a partnership that won't involve the two of us moving."

Her brown eyes went as wide as saucers. "Do you mean it, Daddy?"

"Anna is staying in Starlight?" Evie asked with obvious relief.

"We both are," Josh confirmed.

"Is it what you want, too?" Anna clarified. "I've been a little brat about going, but Starlight is where we belong."

Josh smiled. His daughter had been giving him grief about the move since last weekend, but he'd chalked it up to nerves.

"It's what I want," he said, then blew out a breath as he thought about what else—whom else—he wanted.

"Do you two want to say goodbye to Kayla before we head down to town? I have a lot of moving plans to undo."

The best friends hugged, two peas in a pod.

"First, we have something to show you," Anna told him. "It's a surprise, so you have to close your eyes."

"Tell me you didn't convince Kayla to help you adopt a dog."

Both girls giggled. "It's not a dog, Uncle Josh," Evie told him.

He closed his eyes and slipped his hand into Anna's while Evie grabbed the other one.

By the downhill path they took, he could tell the girls were leading him to the lake.

"I hope you aren't going to toss me in," he said as he stumbled over a stray stick. "I've already said we're staying in Starlight."

"There's somebody else you need to tell," Anna explained and tugged on his hand to stop his forward progress. "Open your eyes."

Josh did, blinking against the bright sunlight reflecting off the smooth surface of the water. And his mouth dropped open as his gaze took in the scene before him. Ella stood at the edge of the dock behind a makeshift structure with the words "Kissing Booth" painted in red block letters above her.

By the time Josh reached the dock, Ella trembled from head to toe. For a few terrifying moments, she thought he was going to simply walk away after realizing who waited for him at the kissing booth.

At that point, she'd wanted to run away instead

of face potential outright rejection. But she forced herself to stay the course. Anna's encouraging wave bolstered her confidence.

What did she have to lose? Only her heart and her pride. She wouldn't know if she didn't take the chance.

There was no way to win without risking failure. This summer had taught her that. No matter what happened in the next few minutes, she would take that lesson with her for the rest of her life. It was a small consolation given how vulnerable she was about to be.

Josh had already told her he didn't want her. But as much as she liked to think she'd gotten her inner strength from her mother, the streak of stubbornness that ran deep through her veins was all her dad's doing. Or maybe she could give herself a little credit.

"Shouldn't you be on a plane headed for someplace exotic and remote at the moment?" Josh asked when he stood directly in front of the booth.

Ella placed her palms against the cool wood. Rob had helped her and the girls build the structure that morning. She needed something to show Josh how serious she was. Her life might not be an '80s movie, but she could still be the heroine of it.

"Somebody pretty smart taught me that you don't have to go far to find adventure. It's an attitude, not a destination." Josh's nostrils flared, and she quickly continued, "I'm not saying you shouldn't go to California. You're in charge of your future.

You've earned that. I want you to know that whatever your future holds, I want to be a part of it."

She flashed a smile, hoping it conveyed teasing instead of terror. "Besides, we both know you could use more practice." She pointed up at the words above her. "I'd like to officially volunteer for that position." She licked her dry lips. "On a long-term basis." She closed her eyes and took a deep breath. "Pucker up, buttercup."

He laughed but didn't seem to move closer. Okay, that was not at all how she'd planned it. In her mind, it had been smooth and sweet. She'd find the right words to convince him to give her another chance.

She opened her eyes and did her best not to show her embarrassment.

"And you say I need help with my delivery?" One thick brow lifted.

"Okay, so sue me. I'm not a screenwriter. Maybe those weren't the right words, but the thought behind them is what counts, Josh."

"What exactly is that thought?"

"I love you. I know you said it doesn't matter, but it does. I don't give my heart easily. I've been too scared, but I don't want to be scared anymore. I want to be brave with you and for you."

"I knew you should've worn a short skirt," Anna called to Ella from the shore. "Daddy likes a girl with pretty legs."

Josh turned and gave his daughter a long stare. "How do you know that?" he yelled.

"I'm a kid," she shouted back. "Not blind."

"Trying to focus here," Ella said. "Can we please stay on the topic at hand?"

Josh returned his attention to her, his eyes twinkling. Twinkling was good, right? At least better than when his gaze had gone flat during their last conversation.

"Remind me about the topic at hand."

"The fact that I love you." She tried not to let her impatience show.

"What about the fact that you're leaving?"

She shook her head. "I'm not."

"You're staying in Starlight?"

She nodded, then cleared her throat. "Maybe." Her throat constricted until she felt like she might not be able to release the next words. But they were important. He had to know exactly how much he meant to her. "Or maybe I'll move to California. I've avoided claiming a home for a long time, but that's over now. I'm claiming my place in the world. It's with you and Anna." She swallowed, then added, "If you'll have me. I don't care where we are as long as—"

He leaned in and kissed her, cutting off her words. It was the kind of kiss that knocked a girl off her feet and revealed everything she needed to know about his feelings.

In fact, when he finally pulled back she could barely focus. His smile told her that he understood the effect he had on her.

"The student becomes the master," he said with a satisfied chuckle.

She stuck out her tongue. "Ego doesn't suit you."

"You suit me." He kissed her again. "I'm relieved you've just saved me from having to fly halfway around the world to tell you that and convince you to return to Starlight. To make a home with me."

"What do you mean?"

His smile turned sheepish. "I was coming up here today and realized these mountains are the place I belong. And you're the only woman I want to share it with. I was coming to pick up my daughter and then we were going to find you, even if we had to trek through the jungle or the desert to do it."

"Really?" She could hardly believe what he was saying, but the love in his eyes left no doubt in her mind or her heart.

"I love you, Ella. I want the rest of our lives to be an adventure, one we're on together no matter where life takes us or what the future brings. We don't need any more practice, sweetheart. We're perfect just the way we are."

"More perfect with a dog," Anna shouted, then ran forward to join them.

Ella came out from around the booth as Josh wrapped both her and Anna in a tight hug. She glanced toward the shore to see Kayla and Rob standing there with her father, along with Mara, Parker and Evie.

Their families cheered and clapped, and Ella felt

tears running down her cheeks. She'd never before cried happy tears. That was something her mom had always done. Ella remembered poking fun at her for it. Now she let her happiness overflow, knowing she'd found a love to last a lifetime.

Epilogue

"You know I don't do camping," Ella said as she pulled a sleeping bag out of the back of Josh's truck the weekend before Anna's new school year started. "Too many nights sleeping on the ground or a lumpy cot when I worked for Traveling Nurses. Now I want a real mattress."

Josh grinned and brushed a gentle kiss across her lips. "Yet here you are in the wilds of the Cascade Mountains, roughing it. You must really love my kid."

The warmth that had infused Ella's heart since that moment on the dock spread through her entire body. "I do love your kid." She ran her tongue along the seam of Josh's lips. "And you."

"And Rocky," Josh said with a laugh as the newly adopted dog galloped up and shoved his wet nose against Ella's bare leg, causing her to yelp in surprise.

"Verdict's still out on the mutt," she complained but couldn't hide her grin. She'd been smiling ear to ear almost nonstop for the past week, enjoying every tiny moment of the life and love she'd chosen, even a slobbering, overly enthusiastic canine.

Anna had chosen the five-year-old Lab mix from a local shelter and immediately christened him Rocky Road. Neither Josh nor Ella had argued, both charmed by the secret meaning of the name. Yes, things were bound to be a little nutty with the three of them forging ahead to create their own version of a family, but Ella wouldn't have it any other way.

It had been Anna's idea to spend the final weekend of the summer camping. Despite what Ella said about sleeping on a mattress, she loved having this time alone with Josh and his daughter. Their friends and family had been thrilled when they'd made their relationship official, but trusting happiness and love was still new to Ella.

Josh did everything he could to make her feel special and she did her best to do the same for him. It was easy to dote on Anna, and with every day that passed, Ella fell more in love with both Josh and his daughter.

She knew this would have made her mother glad and found that once she opened her heart, it was difficult to imagine why she'd ever been so scared in the first place.

There were no guarantees in life, but Ella intended to savor every moment no matter what came her way.

"Rocky and I are going to gather sticks so we can build a fire later," Anna called, waving to Josh and Ella as the dog trotted her way.

"Get lots of them," Ella told the girl. "I want to roast an entire bag of marshmallows."

"Me, too!" Anna let out a whoop of delight, then turned and headed into the trees.

"An entire bag?" Josh raised a brow. "You and Anna are a dangerous combination, and you're both going to wind up with a stomachache."

"Will you kiss it and make it better?" Ella asked as she dropped the sleeping bag into the pile of gear and wound her arms around Josh's neck.

"Always," he promised and kissed her again.

It was a promise she intended to hold him to and offer him in return. Now that she'd found a love to last a lifetime, she was never going to let go.

As they set up the tent, a shimmer of yellow caught Ella's gaze. A small butterfly alighted from a bush at the edge of the clearing, flying high into the air and disappearing against the blue of the late summer sky.

Ella swallowed as her heart tightened with emotion. She understood now that her mother would always be with her, watching over Ella and the ones she loved. She'd learned this summer that allowing herself to truly embrace life was the greatest adventure, and it was a lesson she'd carry with her every day going forward.

* * * * *

And don't miss these other swoon-worthy single parent romances:

The Triplets' Secret Wish
By Cathy Gillen Thacker

Heir to the Ranch
By Melissa Senate

The Little Matchmaker
By Catherine Mann

*Available now wherever
Harlequin Special Edition
books and ebooks are sold!*

WE HOPE YOU ENJOYED
THIS BOOK FROM

SPECIAL
EDITION

Believe in love. Overcome obstacles. Find happiness.

Relate to finding comfort and strength in the
support of loved ones and enjoy the journey
no matter what life throws your way.

6 NEW BOOKS AVAILABLE EVERY MONTH!

#2917 SUMMER NIGHTS WITH THE MAVERICK
Montana Mavericks: Brothers & Broncos • by Christine Rimmer
Ever since rancher Weston Abernathy rescued waitress Everlee Roberts at Doug's Bar, he can't get her off his mind. But the spirited single mom has no interest in a casual relationship, and Wes isn't seeking commitment. As the temperature rises, Evy feels the heat, too, tempting her to throw her hat in the ring regardless of what it might cost her heart...

#2918 A DOUBLE DOSE OF HAPPINESS
Furever Yours • by Teri Wilson
With three-year-old twins to raise, Ian Parson hires Rachel Gray hoping she'll solve all their problems. And soon the nanny is working wonders with his girls...and Ian. Rachel even has him agreeing to adopt a dog and cat because the twins love them. He's laughing, smiling and falling in love again. But will Ian need a double dose of courage to ask Rachel to stay...as his wife?

#2919 MATCHED BY MASALA
Once Upon a Wedding • by Mona Shroff
One impetuous kiss has turned up the heat on chef Amar Virani's feelings for Divya Shah. He's been in love with her since high school, but a painful tragedy keeps Amar from revealing his true emotions. While they work side by side in her food truck, Divya is tempted to step outside her comfort zone and take a chance on Amar—even if it means risking more than her heart.

#2920 THE RANCHER'S FULL HOUSE
Texas Cowboys & K-9s • by Sasha Summers
Buzz Lafferty's "no kids" policy is to protect his heart. But Jenna Morris sends Buzz's pulse into overdrive. The beautiful teacher is raising her four young siblings... and that's t-r-o-u-b-l-e. If only Jenna's fiery kisses didn't feel so darn right—and her precocious siblings weren't so darn lovable. Maybe it's time for the Morris party of five to become a Lafferty party of six...

#2921 WHAT TO EXPECT WHEN SHE'S EXPECTING
Sutter Creek, Montana • by Laurel Greer
Since childhood, firefighter Graydon Halloran has been secretly in love with Alejandra Brooks Flores. Now, with Aleja working nearby, it's becoming impossible for Gray to hide his feelings. But Aleja's situation is complicated. She's pregnant with IUI twins and she isn't looking for love. Can Gray convince his lifelong crush that he can make her dreams come true?

#2922 RIVALS AT LOVE CREEK
Seven Brides for Seven Brothers • by Michelle Lindo-Rice
When a cheating scandal rocks Shanna Jacobs's school, she's put under the supervision of her ex, Lynx Harrington—who wants the same superintendent job. Maybe their fledgling partnership will make the grade after all?

SPECIAL EXCERPT FROM

HQN

*Stationed in her hometown of Port Serenity, coast guard
captain Skylar Beaumont is determined to tough out
this less-than-ideal assignment until her transfer goes
through. Then she crashes into Dex Wakefield. She
hasn't spoken to her secret high school boyfriend in six
years—not since he broke her heart before graduation.
But when old feelings resurface, will the truth bring
them back together?*

Read on for a sneak peek at
Sweet Home Alaska,
the first book in USA TODAY *bestselling author
Jennifer Snow's Wild Coast series.*

Everything looked exactly the same as the day she'd left.

Though her pulse raced as she approached the marina and the
nondescript coast guard station, her heart swelled with pride at the
sight of the *Starlight* docked there. With its deep V, double chine
hull and all-aluminum construction, the forty-five-foot response
boat was designed for speed and stability in various weather
conditions. Twin diesel engines with waterjet propulsion eliminated
the need for propellers under the boat, making it safer in missions
where they needed to rescue a person overboard. Combined with
its self-righting capability to help with capsizing in rough seas, it
had greater speed and maneuverability than the older vessels. The
boat was the one thing she had total confidence in. And she would
be in charge of it and a crew of five.

The crew was the tougher part. She was determined to gain
their trust and respect. She was eager to show that she was one
of them but also maintain a professional distance. Her father and
grandfather made it look so easy, but she knew this would be her

hardest challenge, to command a crew of familiar faces. People she'd grown up with, people who remembered her as the little girl who'd wear her father's too-big captain hat as she sat in the captain's chair in the pilothouse.

Did that hat finally fit now?

Weaving the rental car along the winding road, and seeing the familiar Wakefield family yacht docked in the marina, her heart pounded. The fifty-footer had always been the most impressive boat in the marina, even now that it was over thirty years old. Its owner, Kurt Wakefield, had lived on the yacht for twenty-five years.

Kurt had died the year before. Skylar peered through the windshield to look at it. Had someone else bought the boat? Large bumpers had been added to the exterior, and pull lines could be seen on deck. She frowned. Had it been turned into some sort of rescue boat?

It wasn't unusual for civilians to aid in searches along the coast when requested, but the yacht was definitely an odd addition. There had never been a Wakefield who had shown interest in civil service to the community…except one.

The man standing on the upper deck now, pulling the lines. Wearing a pair of faded jeans and just a T-shirt, the muscles in his shoulders and back strained as he worked and Skylar's mouth went dry. She slowed the vehicle, unable to look away. Almost as if in slow motion, the man turned and their eyes met. Her breath caught as familiarity registered in his expression.

And unfortunately, the untimely unexpected sight of her ex-boyfriend—Dex Wakefield—had Skylar forgetting to hit the brakes as she reached the edge of the gravel lot next to the dock. Too late, her rental car drove straight off the edge and into the frigid North Pacific Ocean.

Don't miss
Sweet Home Alaska,
available May 2022 wherever
HQN books and ebooks are sold.

HQNBooks.com

"Now, I know the circumstances aren't ideal, but I'm looking forward to working with you."

She appeared to struggle, like she was thinking how to formulate her words. "I wish I was working with you by choice and not circumstance. Not that I would choose to," she said with a chuckle.

"I hear you. If it weren't for this situation, we would still be throwing daggers at each other during leadership meetings."

"Put yourself in my shoes. If you were going through this, how would you feel?" she asked, rubbing her toe into the carpet. "Honest answer."

"I'm not as brave as you are, and I have more pride than common sense."

She blushed and averted her eyes. "I would have resigned if I didn't have a mother and sister to consider. Pride is secondary to priority."

He felt ashamed and got to his feet. He went over to her. "You're right. I'm thinking like a single man. If I were married or had other responsibilities, I'd do what I'd have to and keep my job. I was hoping that Irene—" He stopped, unsure of the etiquette of bringing another woman into the conversation.

"No need to stop on my account. I know you had— have—a life."

Lynx wasn't about to talk about Irene, no matter how cool Shanna claimed she was with it. "I'm ready to fall in love, get married and install the white picket fence."

"How do you know you're ready?" she asked.

He rubbed his chin. "I'm at the brink of where I want to be professionally. I want someone to share my success with me."

"I get it," she said, doing that half-bite thing with her lip again.

Don't miss
Rivals at Love Creek
by Michelle Lindo-Rice,
available July 2022 wherever
Harlequin Special Edition books and ebooks are sold.

Harlequin.com

 **HARLEQUIN**

Heartfelt or thrilling, passionate or uplifting—Harlequin is more than just happily-ever-after.

With twelve different series to choose from and new books available every month, you are sure to find stories that will move you, uplift you, inspire and delight you.